Destiny

Also by Katie Richard

Into The Storm

My Last Hope

Destiny

Katie Richard

Katie Richard LLC

Prologue

I am walking across a large field full of beautiful wild flowers toward an opening in the woods. I am not sure why I am going this way. It's as if a magnet is pulling me in that direction. As I step into the woods, I discover a mother deer and her young lying in a patch of tall grass. They don't seem to be bothered by how close I am. In the distance, rabbits, squirrels, chipmunks, and birds move amid the trees. As I keep walking in the direction that's drawing me forward, I silently wonder why I am here? I must be dreaming.

As if reading my mind, the woods slowly start to thin and reveals another small field and a beautiful, picturesque log home in its center. A large porch, with a long swing on it, wraps around the house, and flowerbeds filled with irises and a multitude of flowers inside stone retaining walls line the front. To the side of the house, sits a large stone birdbath with a small black and white bird bathing inside, and multiple types of bird feeders and a gazebo overlooking a small pond are off to the right.

There is a large row of wood stacked neatly to the left of the house and what looks like a vegetable garden beyond that. I step onto the flat stone walkway that is lined with small torches and draw closer to the house. As I place my second foot down onto the stone path, all the torches alongside the walkway light up one by one leading the way to the home. Taking that as a welcome sign, I keep walking. This place feels familiar even though I know I've never been here before.

As I climb the steps to the log home, my heart beats so fast that the only sound I hear is my own pulse. Up above the doorway, there is a small weathered wooden sign that reads "Destiny". Okay, that's a very strange welcome sign. I wonder what I've gotten myself into as I gently knock on the door. No answer. Great. I knock louder this time and wait. From the other side of the door, muffled footsteps draw near. My heart still races, and my stomach is in my throat. I desperately wipe my sweaty hands on my worn-out jeans.

The door slowly creaks open, and behind it is the most gorgeous man I have ever seen. The sunlight turns his dark hair to chocolate brown and caresses his perfectly angled nose, full-chiseled lips, and square jaw. His deeply genuine smile makes my knees grow weak, but it's his eyes that make my body and mind turn into mush. They are almond shaped with deep emerald green irises, and you could easily get lost in them. As I stand there like a speechless fool drinking in his beauty, he casually leans against the door jam in dark blue jeans and a black t-shirt, his hand still resting on the doorknob. His muscular build stands about half a foot taller than me.

"I have been waiting a long time for you, Sierra," he says in a deep husky voice, and in his eyes, it seems there's longing hidden behind them.

"How do you know who I am?" I manage to choke out.

"There are things about this world you don't understand yet, but my name is Dante Xavier, and I'm just a small part of your destiny." He smiles knowingly.

"What do you mean you're part of my destiny? Where am I?" I'm desperately trying not to freak out, but I worry my composure is starting to crack.

"This is my home, and what I mean by your destiny is that there are things called anima gemella or soul mates in this world, and that's what we are. I have been looking for you for nearly a century. Do you know how hard it is to know that there's somebody out there for you, but they just haven't been brought into this world yet?

It has been an excruciatingly long wait." His smile deepens as he tucks a stray lock of my brown hair behind my ear.

I hold my breath and my fingers ache to touch him. His hand falls back to his side. "No, I don't know what a century feels like." This has to be a dream, a century? There's no way somebody like him would ever be my soul mate, let alone wait for me for nearly a hundred years. Unless he's talking about a previous life?

"Do you feel the pull? I'm sure you did. That's what led you here to me. I must tell you, though, I'm a dreamwalker. Right now you are dreaming, that is the only way I can communicate with you until you are aware of what you are. Only then can you decide who you want to be."

It's hard not to look at his mouth as he's talking because it's so distracting. "So, all this is my imagination running wild?" I ask fidgeting with my fingers.

"No, it's not. This is real, and you will remember our meeting when you wake up. I wanted you to know that I am out there. You just don't see me, but I do watch over you to keep you safe. I would never let anybody or anything harm you." He searches my face.

"How do I not know you if you know so much about me?" What would he need to protect me from?

"There is more to Earth than meets the eye, there's a lot that's hidden in the shadows. I grew up exposed to all that this world has to offer, Sierra. A world I'm hoping you will join me in."

I swallow the saliva that is building in my mouth. What is he talking about? "What do you mean by that?"

"That's all I can say for now," he sighs. "I have something that I'd like you to have." Dante's kind eyes say that he wants to say more, but he doesn't.

"Is it going to disappear when I wake up just like you will?" Why do I feel like I am saying goodbye to somebody I love?

"No, it won't." He reaches in his back pocket and pulls out a large oval necklace on a long silver chain.

The front has an oval emerald that matches his eyes. He gently clasps the necklace behind my neck. He's so close that I can smell him. The scent of sandalwood and cedar is almost too much. I feel like I'm getting a buzz just from his scent.

"It's a protection amulet; it will help keep you safe if I'm not there. All you have to do is wear it. If there is evil close by the necklace will heat up, and I will feel it. The necklace is tied to me by magic. I have a matching one." Dante pulls on the black leather cord that's around his neck to reveal another emerald necklace. "You can also use the amulet to find your way back to me if you wish to do so after you know your true identity. The only thing you have to do is promise me that you will keep the amulet around your neck at all times. Its power will be lost at home in a jewelry box," he adds.

I'm not sure why I believe everything that he's saying, but deep down it feels like my soul knows Dante and trusts him. "I promise, but will I ever see you again?" I don't want him to go.

"Of course, you will. I'm not sure when, though. It all depends on when you have all the knowledge of who and what you are." He rubs the back of his neck. "I will, however, see you in your dreams. And another thing, you can't tell your parents that I visited you in your dreams. I promised your father I wouldn't interfere until he told you about your ancestry." He looks at my mouth as much as I am looking at his.

"What do you mean what I am? You know my dad?" I really don't want to think of my parents right now.

"I'm sorry, but that is all I can say at this time, or I would break my oath to your parents. You must find out on your own," he says cryptically.

"Okay, so how do I explain the necklace?" I shoot back at mystery man.

"If they see it, just explain that you found it at a thrift shop or something but just don't mention me." His eyes soften as he smiles down at me. "This is just a temporary goodbye. I will see you again, hopefully soon."

"I don't want to leave." I may not know this man, but I know that this is where I belong. Being with him feels right. I need to be here.

"I know you don't. I don't want you to go either, but until I see you again…" He caresses the side of my face and closes his eyes as if the sight pains him.

He gently wraps his arms around me, and as he does, I know that he completes me. Without a doubt, I feel whole and at home in his arms. As Dante's looking into my eyes, it's like he can see into my soul. He closes his eyes and starts leaning down toward me. My eyes flutter shut, and the next thing I know, his soft lips graze mine. A slow sensual kiss soon turns into one of desperation, like we can't get enough of each other.

Silence descends around us: the bird's chirping ceases, the wind's rustling dies. I can't feel his arms around me anymore. There's only utter emptiness. I open my eyes and find myself back in my bedroom lying in my bed. My heart is pounding so hard that all I hear is the blood pulsing against my ears. Everything is just the same as when I fell asleep except for one thing. The amulet is still around my neck.

CHAPTER 1

SIERRA

I look around at my bedroom, noticing, other than the amulet, nothing has changed since I went to sleep last night. My clothes are still strewn about my bedroom like a hurricane has recently come through. My heart is slamming in my chest because I know deep down that was no ordinary dream. I can't find a way to rationalize it, though. As I lay in bed, I replay the dream over and over again, trying to figure out where I was and how I got there.

Today is June 21st, my eighteenth birthday. I thought I would feel more empowered to be a grown-up than I do. I currently work at a small bookstore part-time, waiting for some sign that says hey, this is what you should do for the rest of your life, but nothing ever comes. I like working at the store, but it's not all that challenging. It's pretty much the same thing day to day, and it can get pretty boring after a while. I feel like I'm meant to do something big, something that matters.

I look at my alarm clock and realize that I slept a lot longer than I typically do. I toss my blankets off and reluctantly climb out of bed. I head into my bathroom, run a brush through my unruly mess of long brown hair, and trot down the stairs. Both of my parents are sitting at the breakfast nook in the kitchen with big goofy grins on their faces.

"Happy birthday sweetheart!" they both say in unison.

"Thank you, so what do we have planned today?" I stifle a yawn.

"Well, first I would like you to open your birthday card, then we'll decide." My dad nods toward the card on the table.

I sit down on the worn-out blue cushion of our nook and reach for the bright red envelope in the middle. I flip the envelope around and tear it open to reveal a beautiful card inside. It has a picture of the beach and sunset and says "Happy Birthday." I read the inside. "On your birthday may all your wishes come true." In my mother's handwriting on the bottom, it says "You may be an adult now, but you will forever be our little girl. Always remember to aim for the galaxy because you are a shooting star. No matter what life brings, follow your dreams. Love Mom and Dad."

"That's not all." My mom hands over a hundred dollars.

"Awe thank you, Mom and Dad, but you know you didn't have to," I say thankfully.

"We know, but we want you to be able to have fun. This is a very special birthday, and we would like you to remember today. It's not everyday you turn into an adult." My mom winks.

"So, we were planning your birthday with Emma, and we were thinking you and Emma could go out to the mall and get your pedicures done. You've got an appointment at twelve, and it's already paid for..." My dad smirks.

"And after that for dinner, maybe we can get takeout from that Chinese place you like so much and eat all together and then do cake?" My mom suggests.

"Yeah, that sounds great. Thank you so much!" I hug them both.

Then I jump out of my seat knowing I slept late. I dart for the stairs to try to get ready as I juggle my phone to call Emma. Finally, after the third ring she answers.

"HAPPY BIRTHDAY!" she shouts into my ear. "So, are you almost ready for our pedicures?"

"How long have you known?" I ask her, laughing.

"Oh, since last month. Who do you think told them where to schedule it?" she teases, also laughing. Emma has never been able to hide anything from me before, so I'm pretty impressed that she lasted this long without spilling it.

"I'll pick you up in about an hour. I need to jump in the shower."

"K, later," she replies.

I rummage through my closet, grab my favorite blue jeans and my black tank top, and head to the bathroom. As I quickly get undressed to get into the shower, I realize I'm still wearing the necklace. I hesitantly reach to take it off, wondering how there was no way my parents didn't notice it this morning. I'm not big on wearing any jewelry, so if they did notice, they didn't say anything. As I set the amulet down on the cream countertop, I notice an inscription on the back that says Destiny. Last night comes back to me, but I still can't seem to make any sense of it. It couldn't have been a dream if I have the necklace as proof, right? He said I need to find out what I am first, what does that even mean? I've never had a dream that felt as real as that one. Could I have gotten the necklace at a thrift shop? I wonder if Emma will think I'm crazy if I tell her.

Weirdness aside, I take a shower, get dressed, and throw some make-up on. I gently grab the necklace and slide it over my head. The metal is cool against my skin, and the silver chain is so long that my shirt can conceal the amulet. I plan to talk to Emma about last night when I see her.

Downstairs in the living room, I say my goodbyes to my parents and promise yet again that I'll be careful. We go through the same conversation every time I leave. It's very annoying, but I think it gives them comfort to keep warning me: be aware of your surroundings, avoid dimly lit places, and the list goes on and on. I mean, come on, they even insisted I learn to fight. They still nag me on keeping up with my offensive and defensive moves. We spar with each other often.

I finally get out to my truck. It's nothing special, but it gets me from point a to point b and is reliable, which is more than I can say about the weather channel. They said sunny and beautiful today. Yeah, I should've known better. No more than ten seconds after starting my truck, the downpour arrives. It's raining so hard I can barely see our little green mailbox twenty feet away. Yeah, it's really sunny and beautiful. Sighing, I put the truck in drive and slowly pull away from the sidewalk leading to our house.

It usually only takes me about ten minutes to get to Emma's house, but because of the rain, it's a few extra minutes longer. I almost hit this huge scruffy black dog on my way. He came out of nowhere and just ran right in front of me. I'm so glad I didn't hit him, I was able to swerve around him. It gave me quite the scare. Is it my imagination or did the amulet warm against my skin prior to the dog?

"Hey, I'm here. You'll probably want to grab an umbrella on your way out." I text her because there is no way I'm getting out in this downpour.

"K," she replies.

As I sit alone in the truck listening to the rain pelting down on the roof, the dream I had last night seems more and more like a dream and nothing more. This necklace must have come from a thrift store or pawn shop. He felt so real though. I silently curse myself for thinking there could ever be more to this world than meets the eye. I decide not to bother asking Emma about the necklace. If I told her, I would be the butt of her jokes for a very long time. We don't have much time left before she goes across country to college, and I go to Ireland with my parents to visit my aunt and uncle. I don't need her to think that I can't handle life without her here by my side. I'm having a hard enough time trying to figure that one out on my own. We've been best friends since the first grade and inseparable ever since.

A loud rapping makes me snap my head up and realize that there is a pissed-off looking Emma banging on the passenger side window. I quickly press the unlock button, and she hops in with rain dripping off her umbrella and all over the truck's floorboards.

"What the hell, Sierra, you knew I was coming right out!" She sounds mad, but I know better. It'll all blow over soon. She's patting down her long straight blonde hair while she looks in the mirror.

"I'm sorry I was spacing." I reach under my tank top and pull out my necklace and hold it out to her. "Do you remember where I got this from?" I decide to go for it anyway. She looks puzzled at it, and then she starts to laugh.

"Is that what you were spacing about, trying to figure out where you got some old-world relic? No, I don't remember when or where you got that from. In fact, this is the first time I've ever seen it." She squishes her perfectly plucked eyebrows together as she gazes at the amulet.

"Oh, all right. No, I was spacing because my parents gave me one hundred dollars for my birthday, and I don't know what I want!" I laugh to cover up my unease. I usually only go shopping with her, if she wasn't with me who was?

"We could check out the mall and see if there's anything that catches your eye, maybe some new outfits. You haven't gotten any new clothes in a while." She glances at my jeans and tank top with that judgmental look of hers.

Somehow, I knew it would turn into makeover Sierra again. I love Emma, I really do. She's my best friend, but she's one of those fashion-conscious girls who always needs the best of everything from the shoes to the purse even to the designer socks she wears. Me not so fashion conscious. I'm more of a pair of jeans and a t-shirt type regardless of where they came from. As long as they're comfortable, that's all that matters. If the occasion arises that I need to wear a dress, I will. I'm not saying I don't enjoy dressing up once in a while. I just need a reason to.

The rain finally starts to slow down to a light sprinkle as we enter the parking garage to the mall. For a Saturday, there aren't too many cars here, so hopefully, we can go shopping without having to fight to get through the aisles. I hate shopping when it's busy. When we finally reach Runway Nail Salon, we decide to get matching French nails. We sit side by side in the very last two massage chairs with the magazine bin in between them. Every time we come here, we sit in the last two seats, so we can talk without really being overheard by the nosy nail technicians.

"You're coming over to my place to stay the night tonight. My parents are out of town for some meeting, so we have the whole place to ourselves," Emma says to me with a wink, grabbing for one of the magazines between us.

"How many people did you invite this time?" I ask in exasperation. It never fails every year she tries to plan a surprise party for me, and set me up with some guy.

"Just a few. My brother, Eric, also invited some friends for you." She grins.

"I told you before I'm not interested in being hooked up with some random person," I grumble.

"Oh, come on, you and Jake broke up a while ago. It's time you put yourself out there more." She rolls the magazine into a cylinder and snaps the end against my knee to make her point.

"And you think Eric's drunken friends are a great match for me? Thanks." I can't believe she brought up Jake. I still feel bad for breaking up with him. He was a really great guy, super attractive, and with a good head on his shoulders. We went out for a while, but it never seemed to grow into anything more than friends, for me anyway. Which is too bad because he was exactly the type of guy I should want.

"No, not necessarily, but some of them are pretty hot," Emma insists raising her eyebrows.

"I'm looking for more than hot. They actually have to have some common sense." Emma's boyfriend, Carl, is captain of our football team. He's your typical jock, hot and arrogant. Carl and Jake were good friends, so it's been hard to be around Carl with all of his snide remarks toward me. I know he resents me for breaking up with Jake.

"You're always quick to find flaws with every guy I point out for you."

"I know what I'm looking for, so why waste my time with the ones that aren't for me?" I shrug.

"Instead of wasting time, why not think of it as passing the time with them?" Emma gives me a mischievous look.

I drop the subject. No matter how many times I say no to her, she's always trying to match me up with somebody. The last blind date she set me up on was with a guy who was a total creeper. I did circles around my block on the way home to make sure he didn't follow me. Just thinking about that guy makes the hair on my neck raise.

Sighing, I grab a Cosmopolitan magazine to read while the nail technician starts on my nails.

I have always had ticklish feet, so it's hard for me not to squirm while they're touching the bottom of my foot. Having a magazine or something to distract me helps. I try not to squirm as she uses the file on my heel, but I do. She gives me a knowing smile. I bet she sees this a lot. But I still apologize anyways.

Once our nails are done, we decide to grab something to eat at the small restaurant inside the mall's cafeteria called Joe's Burgers. We each order a cheeseburger, onion rings, and a drink. This place makes the most amazing cheeseburgers. As we wait for our orders to be filled, we people watch. This became one of our new habits last year. We sit at a little red booth in the corner and watch as the kids run around the mall driving their parents crazy. I remember Emma and I did that when we were young; we were always happy and excited over something so small.

It's not that I'm not happy with my life. I have two wonderful parents, a few good friends, and I do great in school. I have a job though it's not what I picture myself doing in the future. At least it's something. I just have this feeling that I'm meant to do more in this world, that there truly is a destiny for me. My destiny may not be that unnaturally gorgeous man I saw in my dream, but that dream made me open my eyes a little more. I'm an adult now and should act like one.

The waiter finally decides to bring our food out to us, and we both dig in right off. With the crazy morning I had, I completely forgot to eat breakfast, so by now I'm starving. We eat our meals in silence. As I'm finishing the last of my diet Pepsi, I look across the room. My gaze finds an unmistakable pair of deep emerald eyes. It's Dante. Shocked, I drop my cup, and the last remaining soda spills out onto the table. Emma jumps up.

"Crap, I didn't spill any on you, did I?"

"No, what's wrong with you today?" Emma reaches for the napkins to help clean up.

"I don't know." I look up to find that he's gone. I glance around the large open cafeteria and the surrounding areas, but he's nowhere.

"Well, you better start spilling what's going on, or I'll have Carl get it out of you." She narrows her pretty blue eyes at me.

"I promise I'll tell you but not here, okay? When we get to your place." I silently curse myself for saying that. She's very persistent; she won't stop until I tell her everything. How can I explain it to her without her labeling me as a lunatic? I glance around the cafeteria again, desperately trying to find him. After searching all the tables and booths and out into the open area of the mall, I still find no sign of him. I rub my eyes. They must be playing tricks on me. He's not here. Maybe I am turning into a crazy person after all.

DANTE

When Sierra finally arrived in this world. I knew I had to go to her. There was no way that I could hold back any longer. I never really understood the whole anima gemella thing they talked about at the Guardian Academy, until then. I've dated others, but there was never any real spark or connection. I knew the moment Sierra was born; I could feel something different in my heart. There has always been a missing piece, an emptiness inside of me that I never knew was there until the moment she was born. I didn't understand what that feeling was until I snuck into the Colorado Medical Center that night and watched her sleep.

Creepy as it may sound that I was tied to an infant in that way, it wasn't like that, not until she was older. The hospital was pretty easy to maneuver around all the security guards, besides the fact that I planted the thought in their heads that I was also a guard. Humans are so easily manipulated, it's no wonder they need us to protect them. I stood on the outside of the newborn care unit with only the glass separating us. I didn't have to see her name on the little pink card to know. She was known as Sierra Rose Walker, and I would lay down my life to save her. They must have made a mistake on the name card because the staff wrote Wilson instead of Walker.

I was curious as to why she was in a human hospital. Immortals are always born in Graystone. Shortly after her arrival, I did a lot of research on her parents and found out the truth, or at least what the records said in the library. Her father, Michael Walker, and her mother, Sophia Walker, were descendants of some of the most powerful immortal guardians in our history. They were legendary. Sophia, Michael and his brother, Joseph, approached the High Council one day to inform them of the intentions of a man they called Excalibur.

Excalibur apparently had propositioned Michael and Joseph in the hopes of gaining more warriors to join his group he called the Revolution. According to what was written in the statement by Michael, Sophia and Joseph, the Revolution believed that all the immortals, as well as the dark ones, should not have to hide their true nature from the humans. In fact, the humans should be the ones enslaved by the immortals, Excalibur planned to overthrow the High Council. Michael, Sophia and Joseph not only refused to join Excalibur's group of rebels but also, as any good immortal guardians would do, they reported him to the High Council for treason.

After they told the High Council the laws that Excalibur and his group of followers were breaking, Michael and his family started to receive threats. Most of the threats came through fire messages that are sent from a witch or warlock that burn to ash after being read. Some letters were found on their doorstep that went through the mail in Graystone. All of the notes had one of two types of messages, one either join the Revolution or face death, or two you will pay for reporting the Revolution's plan. The High Council would not offer protection to them from the rogue immortal Excalibur, even going so far as to claim that there is no immortal on record whose name is Excalibur. The High Council informed Michael and his brother that they could not find any evidence to justify having a protection guard. The letters were just that, letters with no action.

Within a month of reporting Excalibur to the High Council, Michael and Joseph's parents were murdered in none other than Graystone, the home of the High Council and thousands of immortals. Only the High Council's investigation showed that they committed suicide. Only immortals, warlocks, and witches could gain access to Graystone through a wand shaped blue benitoite portal stone and a sapphire allegiance ring. After their parents' death, Michael, his newly wed Sophia, and his brother fled Graystone, not to be seen in the immortal country again.

Because the High Council assumed that Michael, Joseph and Sophia left with no intention of coming back. They were no longer immortal guardians and the High Council pretty much cast them aside like the deserters they believed they were.

Of course, knowing the High Council, I'm sure that they kept tabs on them. I strongly believe in the High Council and the laws that are set forth for our kind, but there are some things that do not add up. The council's statements do not reveal how they died but simply list suicide. If Michael's parents were indeed murdered by Excalibur, then by law the High Council should have sought justice against him by the High Court. There are no documents in the library suggesting any justice against him. I also could not find out Excalibur's identity. There are no other documents or records with that name on them. It's almost as if he was a ghost.

As Sierra grew up, I watched over her, always staying in the shadows like a guardian angel. I know her parents had to have known I was there, but they never tried to make any contact. It wasn't until Sierra was about seventeen that I finally approached her mother and father while she was in school. They told me what I already knew from watching them. Sierra had no knowledge of being an immortal; she knew nothing beyond the world of humans, not even her real last name. They only agreed to tell me this because they knew I was her anima gemella, although I don't know how they knew that.

I personally thought it was wrong for them not to tell her as a child that it was her duty to protect the humans from the dark ones and keep the world balanced. Her parents did inform me that they would tell her everything she needed to know, and if she wanted to embrace the immortal life or not that it was entirely up to her to decide. They said she would know by the time she had to make the decision. She only had until the end of her nineteenth year. After that, it would be too risky to try to go through the transition. I vividly recall what her father said to me.

"If you get too close to my daughter or try to inform her before we tell her, you will not live to see another sunrise. This decision has to be hers and only hers to decide."

That threat stayed with me always. Watching Sierra's life from a distance I knew her father was never the type to go back on his word. I gave Michael my oath that I would not tell her, and so, I stuck to the shadows. Since I am a dreamwalker, over the years I was able to visit her in her dreams, but as painful as it was, I had to remove Sierra's memories each time. She could never know I was there. I forced myself to be patient and give her parents the time to explain everything. On her eighteenth birthday was the first time I made contact with her and I left her memories intact. She is technically an adult by human standards. But by immortal standards, she became fully mature at sixteen.

Last night I constructed the same dream as always, but this time I gave her the amulet that I had made to help protect her. Through this amulet, I can feel her emotions if they are strong enough, as well as provide a small amount of protection from any demons. While she's wearing it, no demon can touch her without causing themselves great pain. Should any evil forces be in close proximity to her, whether it be demon or dark one, I will know because my matching amulet will start to get very hot against my skin, and so will hers.

I'm glad I gave that to her last night.

The following morning, I feel it, the amulet starting to burn my chest, and an indescribable feeling sweeps through me that something is wrong. I quickly take out my wand shaped blue benitoite stone from my pocket, point it toward the ground with both hands wrapped around it and think of Sierra. I slowly separate my hands to stretch the portal until it is large enough for me to fit through. Her truck is driving down the winding road. Once I step into the small doorway and my boots hit the ground on the other side, I smell it. There is a werewolf following her truck. I bring my hands back together to close the portal and put the wand back in my pocket.

The werewolf gains ground on the truck and runs in front of it, causing Sierra to slam on the brakes. I catch up to him on the side of the road, grab him from behind and fling him into the bushes. As I jump on top of him with my dagger in my hand, his jaw closes around my other arm. His teeth pierce my skin. A burning sensation goes through my veins, and I growl. I grip my silver-coated weapon and stab it as hard as I can into his leg and watch as he turns from beast to man. I drag his unconscious body to a nearby tree. Using my iron handcuffs, I wrap his arms around the base of a tree and bind his wrists together. He isn't going anywhere, and this will buy me time to make sure there are no others.

I roll my sleeve up to inspect the damage. The wound is already starting to heal on its own, the benefits of being an immortal. From the shadows, I then follow her all the way to Emma's house without picking up any other traces of werewolves. Usually, if there is one, there are others lurking about, unless this one was a rogue. Assured that Sierra is safe, I backtrack to the werewolf tied to the tree. He will travel with me to Graystone to answer for his crimes. Werewolves can't be in their wolf form in front of humans, but he was also chasing her truck. I'll check in on Sierra later if I can.

Why would the werewolf run in front of her? Was he trying to make her crash? It sure seemed like it, but why her?

CHAPTER 2

EMMA

We finish picking up after eating and head toward the other end of the mall that we haven't visited yet. This section is where most of the clothing shops are. I can tell that something is bothering Sierra. She's not usually this jumpy or quiet. I'm sure part of that is me leaving Colorado. I chose to go to college across the country, so I could get a break from my family, but also because Carl got a scholarship to play football for North Carolina State University and would be too far away.

The college has a good veterinary medicine program, so my parents weren't too upset about the move. At least I'm sticking with the family business in the medical field. My dad is a doctor, my mom is a nurse, and my brother, Eric, is going to medical school to become a doctor and help with my dad's practice.

Sierra is leaving at the end of next month to go to Ireland. That means we only have about a month left before Sierra leaves, so I don't want to make her more upset than she already is. Maybe it's hitting her today how little time we have left. After she comes back from her vacation, I will be leaving a week later for school.

We visit a bunch of different stores, and I'm able to talk her into this cute red minidress that'll drive the guys crazy tonight. Before I know, it's almost four. People will start showing up at my place around six thirty so we need to get a move on. We walk to the other end of the mall where the parking garage is, put all of our bags in the back seat, and we're on our way.

We stop by the little Chinese restaurant on Fifth Street called The Wok to pick up the order Sierra called in when we left the mall. The restaurant is tiny, but as soon as you walk through the doors, it feels like you've been transported to China. They have beautiful decorations all over the place like dragons, tapestries, paintings, and lanterns hanging from the ceiling. The food here is amazing. It's the only place we go for authentic Chinese food. I'll miss this place when I leave for North Carolina.

When we get back in the truck with the food, I wonder if Sierra and Eric will finally date once I'm not around. I know they both want to, but I'm afraid Eric will break her heart. He's too much of a player to settle with one person, even if that person is Sierra.

The clouds finally start clearing off the closer we get to Sierra's house. I've always loved her mom and dad. They were always like a second set of parents to me. Mine have always traveled a lot for work, so I have stayed at their place many times while my parents were gone.

"Emma, it's great to see you. How's your family doing?" Michael asks after we step into the house and walk into the kitchen.

"They're doing good, working a lot as usual, though," I reply.

"Thank you for helping us surprise Sierra. We couldn't have done it without you." Sophia leans in for a hug.

"No problem, anything for my girl!" I gush as I set down the take-out bags on the black granite countertop.

We eat our delicious meal at the breakfast nook in the kitchen and sing the traditional happy birthday song to Sierra. Her cake turns out to be beautiful. It's one of those photo cakes with a picture of the ocean. She has always loved the water ever since she was little. It's almost sad to put candles into it and cut it up. But after she manages to blow out all 18 candles and we eat the cake. It was definitely worth chopping it up. The cake was delicious and not too sweet like a lot of the pre-made cakes are. I wonder what she wished for this year?

We say our goodbyes to her parents and head out to the truck to go to my place. We make pretty good time. It's about five thirty, which should give us enough time to get dressed and dolled up before everyone shows up.

SIERRA

The ride to Emma's place from my house is a quiet one. Emma knows there's something I haven't told her, and that bothers her. It troubles me too, because we always tell each other everything regardless of how simple it is. I'm having a hard time thinking the dream is real, and it happened to me. She's probably just going to think I'm losing my mind, which rightfully could be true. I keep trying to think of the best way to explain it to her, but there is none. I pull onto the gated road that belongs to her condo building and slowly approach the gate with my little blue Dodge Dakota.

The guard working tonight is an older gentleman with graying hair and tired eyes. He easily recognizes us and lets us through with just a wave of his hand. I make my way to the front of Emma's parents' condo and park the truck. It's a cute yellow building with a concrete walkway leading to the front steps. Before I even get out, she starts in.

"Spill it," Emma demands turning her body toward mine.

I take a deep breath in and slowly exhale. "I don't want you to think I'm crazy, though, so hear me out, okay?"

"I'll be the judge of crazy. Just spill it already." Emma's brows crease in annoyance.

I tell her everything about the dream, not leaving anything out, as well as that I think I saw him at the mall.

"He sounds hot. Why can't I dream about men that look like that," she says in amusement.

"Seriously, Emma I'm freaking out right now," I say, glaring at her for thinking this is a joke.

"Okay, okay." Emma's not trying to hide her humor. "What do you think it means?"

I look down at the amulet for the answer. "I don't know. Do you think I should ask my mom?"

"Absolutely not. If he is for real, and I'm not saying your crazy or anything, but if he is real, he did say not to." Emma shakes her head back and forth.

"What could he mean by saying when I'm aware of who I am though, am I some freak show or something?"

"I don't think so. I would have known," she says chuckling.

"It's not funny. None of this is funny." I cross my arms over my chest. "I only told you so you can help me figure this out."

"I didn't say it was funny. Maybe you are royalty and your parents abducted you. What's not to say that since you're eighteen now, you could be a princess or even a queen. You could be a modern-day *Rapunzel*." She bows a little awkwardly in my truck.

"Really, Emma? So much for not thinking it was funny," I scold her as I throw my empty soda bottle at her. She ducks and the bottle lands harmlessly on the floor by her feet.

"You know what you need, a drink? Let's get in there, and we can start this party early!" She sounds excited at that thought.

I grudgingly get out of the truck and follow her toward the building. While we are walking up the concrete walkway, I look down at my black sneakers to avoid looking at Emma. She's finding humor at the expense of my sanity. It seems like it takes ages for us to get to the door. Once we reach the top step, I plead with her.

"Please don't tell Eric or Carl. Don't tell anybody until we figure this out, all right?"

"I won't," she says quietly.

"Promise me."

"I promise." She smiles and grabs hold of me and pulls me in for a hug.

"Thank you." I hug her back.

She looks at me with a smirk.

"What?" I ask.

"No more crazy talk for tonight, okay, Destiny?" Laughing, she fumbles for her keys.

"Don't start." I knew she would find a way to tease me about this. I can't stay mad at her, though. I would probably react the same way.

Finally inside her condo, I am able to relax a little bit, that is until Eric comes around the corner. I have always had a crush on Eric; he has the bad boy image, which is amazing on him. There are times when he treats me like his little sister, but there have been other times when I thought it was something more. I don't push it. He is Emma's older brother, and I couldn't stand the thought of losing her as a best friend. Emma walks away to use the restroom and leaves me alone with Eric.

"Happy birthday beautiful!" He beams as he jogs up to me and lifts me up to spin me around in a circle. He gently sets me back down on my feet again.

"Thank you, Eric," I say a little shyly, looking into his deep blue eyes. It's not like him to be this forward, with me anyway. Sure enough, somebody ruins it by clearing their throat.

"I brought some friends to celebrate your birthday. This is Taylor, Ryan, and Casey." Eric gestures to the three-frat boys beside him. We exchange hellos, but I'm not really interested in getting to know any of them. My eyes keep straying to Eric.

Emma finally emerges out of the bathroom and waves for me to follow her to her room. I grab all of my bags and head up the stairs to where all the bedrooms are. I look at all the family pictures hanging on the wall leading up the staircase, but the face I keep finding in whichever picture I look at is Eric's. His deep blue eyes are striking with his black hair. I walk into Emma's bright green room plastered with posters of boy bands and shirtless guys and toss my bags on the floor in the corner of her room.

"Are you ready?" she asks, almost giddy with excitement.

"Ready for what exactly?" I back away a little wary.

"I am going to make you look irresistible!" she says proudly.

"You don't need to do that, you know. I'm not into the frat boys downstairs." Here we go again.

"For one, you just met them, so you can't say that for sure, and for two, I know of one you are into." She gives me a smile that says she knows the truth.

"Really, who?" I challenge.

"Eric, and don't try to deny it. I've seen the way you look at him."

"He's hot. I can't help it, but he's your brother," I say defensively, putting my hands up.

"I know he likes you. I overheard him talking to his friends earlier about you," she admits as she wiggles her eyebrows.

"The answer is no; he's your brother, so he's off-limits." I quickly try to cut her off.

"And why do you say that?" She's shaking her head back and forth, closing her eyes.

"Because if it ended badly, which I'm sure it would, I wouldn't want you stuck in the middle. It's not worth our friendship." It's almost like I'm trying to tell myself this.

"Do you seriously think I would let it hurt our friendship? Not a chance." She starts rummaging through my bags of new clothes. "This is what you will wear." She states like a fact, holding up my new strapless red mini dress. "Eric won't have a chance, trust me."

What the hell. Why not? I shimmy out of my tank top and jeans. Why not look good tonight? The red mini dress fits my curves perfectly and makes my bust line look fuller.

As I redo my make-up, Emma brings me my black pumps and begins going through her own wardrobe. She picks out a black halter dress and winks at me. She dresses like she's going out to a club on most days, so it's not out of the norm for her, but for me, I only dress like this once in a while, and it's usually because she talked me into it. It's not that I dislike being girly. I just prefer more practical clothes like pants with pockets.

"Is Carl coming tonight?" I already know the answer.

"Yeah, he'll be here in about an hour." She quickly swaps her clothes.

I take a deep breath. "Are you going to abandon me out there?"

"No, I wouldn't do that to you," she says, covering her heart with her hand, acting all innocent.

"Bullshit, you wouldn't. You've done it before. Many times, in fact!" I remind her.

"Oh, it wouldn't be for long. Besides, quality time with them wouldn't be a bad thing, you know, especially after the day you've had. Amanda, Kayla, and Cynthia are coming too. So, you wouldn't be on your own."

As we walk down the stairs, Emma in front of me, the catcalls and whistles begin. I honestly didn't see the sense in getting dressed up to stay inside, but Emma knew what I needed. To feel good about myself. Her motivations for wanting me to hook up with her brother were probably the same. Wanting me to forget my day and the fact that my parents could be hiding something. I can feel my smile getting broader and broader with every step I take.

"I need a drink," I say, laughing as the four guys are bowing before us on the last step. How dramatic.

"Yes, I believe a drink is in order for the birthday girl. What do you want?" Eric replies as he looks me up and down.

Now that's a loaded question, but I figure my best option is choosing a drink. "Strawberry daiquiri, please." Eric has always made phenomenal daiquiris.

"Coming right up." He gives me a big grin before he turns and sways back and forth on his way to the kitchen. I silently wonder how much he drank before the party even started. He has always been quite the drinker. Which only got worse when he enrolled in college. He's going to medical school to be a doctor. I'm not sure why he would want to help his dad, though. When the two get together, there seems to be a lot of tension between them. Maybe that's because they're both strong-minded people.

"I'll take one too," Emma chimes in.

The five of us head to the basement, which is where Emma and I usually spend most of our time hanging out. The "party room" takes up the whole basement, and the kids have always had free reign of it. There are three large black leather couches arranged around a big-screen TV connected to pretty much any type of gaming system you could ever imagine. There's a decent size dance floor on the other side of the room with a polished wood floor—Emma's idea. Eric, on the other hand is the proud owner of the large pool table that he consistently wins bets on.

This is where they've always thrown parties; their parents figured if the kids had the basement, the rest of the house wouldn't get trashed. Her parents are more laid back than mine. They don't care if there are parties while they're out of town. Their only rules are that nothing upstairs gets broken, and absolutely nobody is allowed in her dad's office. The three guys head over to the pool table and set their beers on the side table.

"Special delivery!" Eric announces as he comes down the stairs.

"Some delivery boy you are! I expected my drink here like yesterday," Emma says, shaking her finger at him. "See if you get a tip."

"Man, delivery man. And I'm the best damn looking delivery man there is, so forgive me for my one flaw in being late," he says as he hands me my drink. His gaze rests on my mouth. "Isn't that right, Sierra?"

"Well, you are the best-looking guy I've seen, although I haven't seen too many," I joke, trying to remove some of the tension building up inside me.

"Ouch, wow you know how to hurt a man, Ms. Wilson," Eric says as he feigns a broken heart. The other guys can't hold back their laughter, and they let him hear it.

The doorbell ringing interrupts whatever he was about to say. Emma goes upstairs to get the door. While she's away, I awkwardly stand there not knowing what to say to Eric, so I just sip my daiquiri. A few moments later, Emma comes back down into the basement with Carl, Amanda, Kayla, and Cynthia in tow.

The night goes on pretty uneventful: we play pool, do some dancing, and drink more than we should. The tension is definitely there between Carl and I, so I'm actually grateful when he and Emma sneak off. During the next hour, I'm finding the more I drink, the more the dream seems just a dream. Maybe I did get the amulet at a thrift shop, and some crazy lady did some voodoo to it. Eric and I start flirting quite a bit back and forth. Until now, I didn't realize just how much I'll miss our banter once Emma leaves for college. It'll be odd for me to come over to just visit Eric, wouldn't it?

I go upstairs to use the restroom, swaying a bit as I walk. After I go to the bathroom for like the tenth time tonight, I check myself in the mirror. Although flushed, I still look like me, no noticeable changes into adulthood. I do look good in this dress if I do say so myself. I turn the doorknob and push the door open to find Eric on the other side.

"Ah!" I jump. "What the hell, Eric!"

"I'm sorry I didn't mean to scare you." He reaches for my hands. He puts both of them in his. "Do you know how beautiful you are?"

"Yup, you are drunk for sure," I say. This is very odd behavior for Eric. Well, toward me anyway. I have seen him do it to countless others.

Before I realize it, he is leaning toward me, and I freeze. I can't believe this is happening. I have wished for this so many times in the past, and it's actually happening. He starts to kiss me and reaches his hands into my hair. His kiss is odd, though. It's hard and forceful, like he's claiming me. I picture Dante's face, it doesn't feel right kissing somebody other than Dante. I gently push him away with my hands on his chest. What the hell is going on with me? Why would I instinctively push Eric back?

"Eric, this isn't a good idea."

"Come on, baby, of course it is. I know you want me," he says, lowering his head toward mine again.

"That may be true but not like this, not drunk." I take a step back. I do want him, but as crazy as it sounds, I want Dante more. I need to feel that fire in my veins that I had when Dante kissed me. I don't feel that with Eric.

"How does that matter?" he retorts, looking like the defiant bad boy that he is.

"It matters to me. If you still feel the same tomorrow..." I say, and I let the sentence hang. Maybe I'll feel different tomorrow too? He can use his imagination to fill in the blanks. I slowly walk away from everything I have always wanted and go back downstairs, wondering if I have made a giant mistake.

It takes a while for Eric to return to the basement, and when he does, he seems strangely quiet. I guess he's not used to being turned down. I know I'm still shocked that I did that as well. He's always been that one that's out of reach. If he rejected me that would completely change our relationship. I've always enjoyed our flirting and have come to expect it, but tonight he seems pushier than normal.

CHAPTER 3

DANTE

It's always been hard for me to watch Sierra with other guys, even though she didn't know about me. I can't blame her. After all, she's a teenager. But this guy, Eric, I've got a really bad vibe from him. I don't know if it's his personality or the way Sierra looks at him, but he feels dangerous. I sense she cares deeply about him, so that doesn't help either. I can't wait for Emma to go to college so Sierra won't have a reason to come here anymore. It seems Emma's parents are always gone, and the kids do whatever they want.

As I check in on her through the window in the dining room, this lowly human kisses my girl. I can't help the fists that clench by my sides. I have to remind myself that I have to protect humans, not harm them. That line has been drawing pretty thin lately. Now that she looks like a beautiful young woman, she has been catching the eyes of many. The worst part is, I don't think she even means to.

Not soon enough, Sierra pushes him away and leaves Eric. My cell phone starts to buzz. I take it out of the front pocket of my black pants, already knowing what the message will say: 271 Maple Street, Sunnyside, Colorado. Just an address that sounds simple enough but is invaluable to my mission. I take out my blue benitoite portal stone and think of none other than 271 Maple Street, Sunnyside, Colorado.

At first, the portal appears like a small flashlight beam emanating from the stone. Gradually I make the doorway larger and larger until I can step through it. As I emerge on the other side of the portal, I'm immediately on edge. I close the portal and put my stone back into my pocket. I sense a demon and more than one of them. An icy air, smelling of rotting flesh, brushes my skin. Both are clear signs a demon is near.

I reach behind me and pull my katana out of the sheath on my back. The weapon was forged in holy water on sacred ground by the Holy Ones, which are the keepers of faith in our species and are the creators of weaponry. This katana has killed more demons than I can count and has proved itself as an irreplaceable piece for me. Wherever I go, my weapons come with me—at least three silver daggers, a half-dozen wooden stakes, and of course, my prized katana.

I look up to see an unremarkable small blue house with white trim. The yard and the flower gardens have grown out of control, so it's obvious the owner hasn't taken very good care of the yard. I edge toward the front door along the side of the property, keeping to the shadows as much as possible, wary of my surroundings. I keep my katana in my right hand ready to strike. I bang my left fist three times on the white front door as I peer inside, looking for anything out of the ordinary. Nobody answers, but muffled voices come from inside. Again, I bang on the door three times shouting, "I am Dante of the immortal guardians. Open the door now, or I will open it with force!"

A small older brunette runs to the door, eases it open a crack, and says, "Can I help you?"

I recognize her from a photo of rogue witches though I cannot recall her name. "I am Dante of the immortal guardians, and I am here under orders from the High Council. There have been reports of demon activity in the area. Most specifically stemming from this address. Have you seen anything out of the ordinary?" I ask, although I already know the answer.

"Demons? Seriously?" She shakes her head and eyes me as if I'm a tad crazy. "No, I haven't. Could be my neighbors." She laughs. "They're a little strange, and always so loud and obnoxious, to the point that it would be easy to imagine them doing something bizarre with the company they keep!"

"May I come in?" I say merely out of politeness. I suspect she's hiding something and trying to get me to focus on her neighbors.

"Uh, no, my house is a mess right now, but I can talk to you out here," she stammers.

"It was not a request, and you know that!" I snap at her. "You are a witch. That means I have the authority to go into your house if I deem it necessary and suspect you are breaking the law by summoning demons!"

"I am not a witch and I most certainly am not summoning demons. On what basis would you think that?" Her voice is shrill, now clearly frantic.

"Get out of the way now, or I will be forced to move you," I say very quietly, not breaking eye contact. She's clearly intimidated by me. She is about half my size, and she keeps looking at the sword in my hand. Witches and warlocks are very strong creatures and may have magical abilities, but they can die just as easily as a werewolf or a vampire. Most witches and warlocks have an allegiance with the immortals, although there are plenty out there that do not.

The easiest way to tell a witch or warlock that is an ally would be the blue sapphire allegiance ring one must wear at all times. Again, these are made from the Holy Ones and allow entry to Graystone. This witch is not wearing one. The rogue witches and warlocks are usually the ones that cause problems like these demon sightings. Though I'm unsure of the real reason they would want to summon a demon. Clearly, some are not very wise.

"Please, you have to understand he's not well," she says with pleading eyes.

"Who is not well?" I demand.

"My husband, Malik." She begins to cry. "He found this book in an old warlock library, and since he started reading it, he's gone mad. Malik is very paranoid and thinks that the world is out to get him, and so he thinks he needs to protect our house."

"By protect, you mean summoning demons?" I ask incredulously, putting my other hand on my waist.

"Only a few, but they are controlled by him through an agreement. They protect us, and in exchange, he will free them from the demon bodies they are bound to so they won't have to be demons any longer," she says with shaking hands, sounding a bit mad herself.

"Are you serious? You know you can never trust a demon!" I shout at her. "I am going to have to take both of you to the High Council for trial. That is after I kill the demons. How many have you summoned?" The veins in my neck are throbbing, my muscles tightening.

"Three, I believe." She's wailing now. "Please don't hurt Malik. He meant no harm."

"You stay here while I deal with the mess you've created." I push the door open wide enough to get a good look inside. The house is a bit messy with books and what looks to be bottles of potions spread haphazardly across the rooms.

As I stride inside, the thud of my black lace-up combat boots on the unpolished hardwood floor echoes into the eerie silence. I have my right fist around the handle of my katana, and I slowly reach into my left boot to grab my dagger, which was also forged by the Holy Ones. The stench thickens the farther I walk into this house. If not for the years of training I have endured, I would be buckled over throwing up by now.

A loud shriek rips into the room from below the floor I'm on. The type of shriek that will raise all the hairs on your neck and have your heart hammering in your chest. That shriek was not any ordinary demon shriek. That was a banshee, notoriously hard to kill due to how quickly they can move. They are one of the fastest demons I've ever fought.

The banshee must be in the basement. Before it kills Malik, I need to find the way down quickly. I don't bother asking the woman any questions. I know she'll lie. I open a wooden door only to find that it's just a pantry stocked with dry goods. I then walk down the narrow hallway, open the next wooden door on my right, and find a staircase that leads to the basement. Boots thudding, I run down the stairs with my katana out in front of me. If that banshee decides to lunge for me, I will be ready. I have been caught off guard by them before, and I'll be damned if that will happen again.

Banshees don't have teeth and claws like other demons because they are more like a ghost of their former self. Although they have become creative in ways to harm or even kill you, the last banshee I fought managed to stab me with a staircase spindle through the thigh. That was not a pleasant experience. But I did learn a hard lesson from it.

In the center of the musty basement, there is a large circle drawn on the floor with chalk. Around that same circle are various summoning symbols. Movement above makes me look up. I suck in a breath. Two banshees hover over a fragile-looking old man. Silently I assess my options; either I can alert them to my presence, or I can take a chance and throw a dagger and hope the old man is spared. The husband may have been the one to summon the creatures, but that doesn't mean he should die for it. It is still my duty to protect him.

"Hey!" I shout. Both banshees whip around with another loud shriek. "Pick on somebody your own size, won't you?"

The banshees both lunge toward me, which I had already planned on. I wait till the last second to squat down and thrust my katana upward with as much force as I can muster in that position. A shriek so loud sounds out that I must try to cover my ears for fear of losing my hearing. The banshee that I hit with my katana is dying, it writhes on the floor in a heap as smoke bellows from its insides. I waste no time and charge the other banshee. She shrieks and pivots at the last moment and darts across the room, far away from the old warlock and me. I want to ask him if he's hurt, but I don't want to take the chance of being distracted.

I pull my gaze away from him in time to see a large metal chest racing toward me. I leap to my right and start to run toward the last banshee, but she grabs a chair from beside her and throws that at me as well. I dart to my left, and as I do, I slip on something wet and fall on the cold hard concrete. My head slams against the floor so hard that I see a flash of bright light in my peripheral vision. Unsteadily I roll onto my knees and push off the floor, feeling light-headed.

"Watch out!" Malik shouts.

I pivot on my heels with my katana out in front of my face in time to see the banshee's look of shock as she realizes she can't stop herself from slamming into my blade. I hold my katana out straight as I lunge for her abdomen—another ear-piercing shriek as she turns to nothing but a cloud of smoke as well. I stand there, katana still outstretched in my hand, trying to ignore the hammering pain in the back of my head. I glance to the right of me to where Malik is and notice just how damaged he looks. His clothes are rumpled, his hair greasy and unkempt, but it's his eyes that tell me the most. He has large dark circles under his wild brown eyes. The skin on his face is so sunken in that it looks as if he hasn't had a meal in weeks.

"You know why I'm here?" I ask.

"To lock me up?" He sniffs and raises his chin up.

"To bring you and your wife into the High Council on the count of summoning demons. Speaking of, where is the other?" Realizing at that moment that I had only dispatched two of the three that his wife said he summoned.

"There is one other," he says cryptically.

"And where is that one?" I'm not liking this game he thinks he can play. After all I did just save his life from the looks of it.

"I don't kn-now," he stammers.

"You don't *know*?" I growl.

"I tried to keep it here, I really did. I just wasn't strong enough," Malik says. "You should know it's... it's not a banshee."

"And what may I ask have you let loose in this world?" I ask, already dreading the possibilities.

"A chimera," he blurts. And with those two small words, I know that I am going to need a better arsenal of weapons for my next battle. I place magical handcuffs on both Malik, and his wife, whom I later find out is named Elizabeth. These handcuffs are made with iron so that any magical being's powers will be useless. I then take out my blue benitoite stone and make a portal to the Guard in Graystone.

ERIC

Why does my life have to be so fucked up? Why can't I just be the guy who wants the girl and not have ulterior motives jammed down my throat? Ever since I was thirteen and found out who my dad truly was my life has been hell. It's no wonder I have to drink so much to numb myself from the hatred I feel toward him and now myself for what I'm being forced to do.

If I don't go along with what Raymond—I don't like thinking of him as my dad—and his associates want me to do, they'll hurt Emma. It really shows how much my dad cares about his kids. To use us as pawns to get what he wants. I can't help how I feel about Sierra. I think deep down, I have always loved her, and that's why I have not been trying really hard to do what my dear old dad wants.

The bad thing about drinking so much is that it makes me let my guard down. I mean, yeah, I still flirt with her when I'm sober, but when I drink, I'm afraid I'll let her in, and I can't have that. It's bad enough I know she likes me. I don't want her in love with me. That'll just hurt her so much more than what I'm already going to have to do to her. But god damn, why did she choose tonight to look this hot? I am glad she turned me down in a way; she deserves better. But what I wouldn't give to just have one night with her without all the rest of the baggage.

I have thought about just taking her and Emma and running away, but I know they would find us. I've already tested that when I brought the girls "camping" a few years ago. Raymond knew exactly where we were even though I borrowed a SUV from a friend he didn't know without all the fancy GPS systems in it. He was still able to pinpoint where we were in Montana. I still haven't figured out how yet, though I suspect Kairos had a hand in that. I hate that warlock.

At least it looks like Sierra is having a good time tonight. I had to step outside and get some air after she turned me down. Well, she did say if I still felt this way in the morning... But I can't take her up on that, as much as I want to. I just have to try to keep myself in line for the rest of the night. In the morning, I'll be more clear-headed. My phone starts ringing in my pocket, and the dread starts to set in. I have this ringtone set for the man I despise the most in this world.

"Hello, Raymond," I reluctantly answer.

"Would it kill you to call me dad?" he replies.

Probably at some point it will. I say aloud, "Maybe you should act like one."

"Not that I have to explain myself to you, boy, but I am doing this for our future," he clips out. I better tread lightly.

"What do you need?" There's always something he wants.

"Have you talked to Sierra about leaving with you yet?"

"No, not yet. I haven't been able to get her alone." Not like that would be high on my priority list when I do.

"Well, you need to get this done soon. The boss is getting antsy. She's 18 now, so she could make the transition," he states this as if it was a foregone conclusion that she wants to.

"I'll do what I can, bye." And I hung up. I didn't give him the chance to reply. My high of kissing Sierra is now officially soured thanks to him.

I don't see why they need Sierra so much, he says that she will prove to be an invaluable asset and for their plan to work they need her. I've never met his boss, but with how scary Raymond can be, if he's intimidated by his boss, he must be pretty badass and not in a good way. I have been to the lab where Raymond spends most of his time being a "doctor," and he's always doing experiments with immortal blood, and sometimes even warlock, fairy, vampire, and god knows what else type of blood. I'm a full immortal because Charlotte is not my biological mom, only Emma's. I have also successfully gone through the agony of the transition. Though Emma doesn't know any of that.

Raymond claims my mother died during childbirth, but I have my doubts. Emma is considered a half-breed because Charlotte's a human, so it is very risky for Emma to try to go through the transition. I think the only reason that Raymond hasn't involved Emma is that if she dies during the transition, he wouldn't have leverage to use against me. Sometimes I wonder if that is the only reason, he had another child. Well, I need another drink to make it through another lovely night of being me.

Several hours later, everybody finally decides to call it a night. Thank god, I was having a really hard time trying to distance myself from Sierra. I don't want to hurt her, but the alcohol is making it hard to remember the reason why I should stay away. If she knew what kind of fucked up person I was, would she still want me? Even though I drank so much tonight, when I finally make it upstairs to my bed, my mind won't stop racing. I keep thinking about that kiss and how I wish there was a way we could be together like a normal couple. But nothing about this is normal.

She's right next door in the spare bedroom. I can always just go talk to her. Tell her how screwed up this world that we live in really is. I can tell her that her parents have been lying to her and she's an immortal too. But would she believe me? I probably wouldn't if I hadn't seen it with my own eyes. I decide to stay in my room and just lay here awake staring at the ceiling while contemplating all the ways I can try to get us all out of this hell I have found us in.

CHAPTER 4

SIERRA

The following morning, I wake up to a killer migraine. I slowly open my eyes to the brightness of the spare room at Emma's. I don't understand why so many people enjoy waking up to the sunlight on their faces. I love the dark; my blackout curtains keep all light out of my room unless I open them. That's how I enjoy waking up, on my own, not from the sun blinding me. I look around the pale pink room and notice that the other girls must have gotten up already or were sleeping in the basement. Last night is kind of foggy. I gingerly get up off the futon, noting that my head weighs what feels like one hundred pounds.

I walk down the hall, and Emma's door is wide open with just Carl passed out on her bed. So, I decide to take the stairs toward the wonderful smell of fresh coffee brewing. Eric is in the kitchen making himself a coffee. It looks like everybody else must still be sleeping since it is just him that I see. Even with ruffled hair and just pajama pants on, he still looks like he could be a model on the front cover of a magazine.

"Good morning, Eric." I struggle not to look too hard at those washboard abs.

"Hey, good morning," he says after he jumps like I startled him.

"Do you know where Emma is?" I ask, trying to avoid looking at him.

"She said she was going to the bakery up the road to get donuts," he sounds more exhausted than I feel. "How did you sleep?" There's genuine concern in his voice. That's something.

"I slept okay, I guess, but my head is pounding. How about you?" This time, I dare to look at him. I don't want to tell him I stayed up much later than everybody else, thinking about him.

"I didn't sleep much, and my head hurts as well. Would you like some coffee?" he asks, changing the subject.

"Yes, definitely thank you." I can't live without coffee. He seems like he's trying to avoid eye contact as well. I guess I know now that it was the alcohol talking last night. I'm glad I turned him down then because I couldn't bear it if he felt ashamed of being with me. Just thinking about that made my cheeks feel warm, and I had to excuse myself to go to the bathroom. I tried splashing cold water on my face to cure the embarrassment I felt of what could've happened. After a few minutes of telling myself I should've known better, I mean, come on he's the male equivalent of a ho. I would just be another notch in his headboard anyway, even if I wanted to be more.

I finally cool my face and my nerves down enough to go back to the kitchen. I try to act indifferent to what might have happened last night as I make my coffee in silence. Minutes later, I escape with it up to the spare bedroom. Hopefully, once the caffeine kicks in I won't feel like such an idiot.

A few moments later, I hear Emma come in the house loudly saying, "Donuts! Come get your fresh donuts!"

I couldn't help but chuckle. Only Emma can make an entrance like that. I figure I better go down there because if I don't, she will think something is wrong and bug me about that. I slowly make my way down the stairs, still sipping on my coffee, as I hear Carl's muffled footsteps coming from behind me.

"Good morning, Carl," I say without looking back.

"Morning," he replies. Typical Carl; he won't say any more to me than he has to.

"Well, good morning, sleeping beauty," Emma says as I arrive at the bottom of the staircase.

"Good morning to you too. You guys were up awfully early today." Emma and Kayla start to open up all the boxes of donuts.

"Only because Carl snores!" Emma giggles. Carl just shrugs his shoulders.

Everybody starts clumsily reaching into the boxes and grabbing what they want. My hand brushes up against somebody's, and I look up and find out its Eric's hand. We lock eyes for about two seconds, and then he hurries away, donut in hand, up the stairs. No doubt to run away from me. When did we become so complicated? He looked rough, though, like he hadn't gotten much sleep last night. I hope I didn't do anything wrong.

After he goes upstairs, Emma looks right at me so I know she saw the exchange. Sure enough, she raises her eyebrows at me as if to say you better tell me everything. I guess it's a good thing I have to work tonight, so I have a good excuse to skip out of here pretty soon. I haven't seen any of Eric's friends yet, and I wonder if they went home last night or crashed downstairs.

For the rest of the time I'm here, Eric stays in his room, which is very odd for him, especially with all these girls in his house. After I help clean up the basement, I decide I should leave. I don't want to make things any harder for him or make him feel like he has to hide in his own house. I don't know when his friends left, but they weren't in the basement when we went down there.

"I'm going to head out. I have to take care of some stuff before I go to work tonight. Thank you for everything, Emma. You're the best. And thank you all for coming. I had a lot of fun." I hug them all besides Carl.

"You're welcome, and call me when you're free." Emma hugs me back.

As I walk out the front door with my shopping bags in my hand and head to my truck, I have this eerie feeling like I'm being watched. I look around but I don't see anybody. I walk a little faster than normal just in case. I chalk it up to the wild past few days I've had. As soon as I shut my truck door, I press the lock button before I start the engine. I finally make it to my driveway, and I can just feel all the tension leave my body. I didn't realize I was that tensed up until I wasn't anymore.

My mom's SUV is gone, and when I get to the door, it's locked, so I have to juggle my bags to dig the house keys out of my little black purse. For such a small purse, it's amazing how things can get lost in there. I can't imagine having a large purse. Once I'm finally opening the door, the security alarm starts its warning beeps. So, I quickly put my code in to turn it off and am kind of relieved to just be alone in the house. I don't have to pretend everything is okay, at least for a little bit. I rearm the alarm since I plan on taking a nice long hot shower to wash away the past few days.

DANTE

I got a call to head toward the northeastern part of Colorado. According to the reports, there are vampires mingling with humans at a local bar and offering them eternal life in exchange for blood. Just like any other dark one, vampires can live amongst the humans but must keep their vampire part to themselves.

There are blood banks where vampires can get blood from humans without having to bite them. We have a deal with the local hospitals where the High Council is a financial donor and in return can get about half of all blood that is donated to them from the humans. They have these set up pretty much anywhere in the world. It shows what having money can get you.

When you can live for hundreds or even thousands of years, you can amass quite the financial power. The High Council is able to get back a portion of what they donate to the blood banks and other organizations from the type of beings that use them. A good example would be a lot of vampires will run nightclubs where a portion of their proceeds will go back to the High Council. Kind of like the way taxes go toward education or infrastructure in some places.

As soon as I walk into the bar, you can tell who the vampires are by the way they look at me. It's like a criminal who sees a police officer. The look of guilt is written all over them. I'm wearing my standard black uniform that is guardian-issued with my weapons on display. Humans don't tend to say much to me about them because I usually plant the seed in their minds that I am supposed to have these. Glamouring a human is a simple thing to do. All it consists of is making eye contact with the human and telling them what to believe, and all immortal guardians have that ability.

I survey the room, trying to find the one they call Chase. He's the one that was reported as the leader of the eastern Colorado area vampire clan. Most states will have multiple leaders of vampire clans depending upon the population. I spot him soon enough with his bleach-blonde hair and pasty white face. As I walk closer to him, he starts moving in the opposite direction. I walk a little faster, so does he. What he doesn't know as he's speeding toward the exit is that Maverick is already there. I'm not an idiot; they always run toward the exit that's farthest from me. They are so predictable it's almost not even a challenge.

I'm following him closely through the crowd as he reaches for the back door and swings it wide open. Maverick is waiting for him with a grin plastered on his face. Maverick is about six foot with black hair and hazel eyes. I don't hear what he says because it's so loud in the club, but I'm good a reading lips, and it looks like he says, "A word, Chase."

Chase steps out the backdoor behind Maverick as I reach him and I shut the door as I trail close behind them both.

"I don't know what your problem is dude. I'm minding my own business just having a good time." It's not hard to see his white fangs in the moonlight while he's talking.

"Is propositioning the locals for a blood trade part of your good time?" Maverick asks.

"What are you talking about?" Chase straightens up defensively, he's trying to play stupid.

Why do they always think playing dumb will work? "Come on, Chase, we know you as well as some members of your clan have been offering humans eternal life so they can use them as blood bags." I keep my hand in my front pocket with a wooden stake in my grip.

"Well, they are blood bags," Chase spits out.

"It's against the laws of the allegiance to feed on a human," I tell him.

"I didn't sign an allegiance, so I'm not bound to your stupid laws," Chase declares, shifting on his feet as if he's ready to bounce.

"Yes, actually you are. You fall under Cassidy's jurisdiction, and she signed the agreement. Therefore, so have you," Maverick reminds him. Cassidy is the vampire clan leader of North America.

"That's bullshit. I didn't sign up to be somebody's little pet," Chase sneers at Maverick.

"You can take that up with her if you like, but there will be no feeding on any humans here," I reiterate, my hand tightening around the stake.

"You can't tell me what to do." Chase curls a lip at me, flashing one of his incisors.

"Well, you can't feed on humans, or I will have to take you to the Guard for punishment," I tell him in a low steady voice, hoping he takes the hint.

"We'll see about that." Chase bolts and runs faster than I can blink an eye toward the end of the alley and snatches a human walking by. We dart after him, with weapons drawn, trying to stop him before he bites her. We're too late, though. He tears into her neck like a lion tearing through their prey. Her blood-curdling scream and thrashing body goes limp before we reach her.

"Let her go, Chase!" I yell to him.

"Drop the human, now!" Maverick shouts as well.

When we get to him, I don't give him the chance to let her go; I stab him in the side above the waist and through his ribs with my wooden stake and as far in as I can go. He pulls back and hisses with his face covered in blood. The victim falls to the ground, not moving. Maverick instantly drops to his knees beside her and applies pressure to her neck, trying to slow the river of blood coming from her. I pull the stake out of his side to another hiss of pain from him.

"What the hell is wrong with you? You got a death wish or something?" I ask him.

"I'm a vampire, and I should be able to be one. Drinking from bags of old stale blood is not a way to live," Chase manages to choke out. Vampires do not heal like us immortals, so the stab wound would continue to bleed like any human. Good, let him bleed. That's what he deserves.

"Regardless, those are the laws, and you broke them. I have to take you in now," I say as I put iron handcuffs around his wrists.

"What about my-my side. I'm go-ing to bleed out," Chase stammers.

We could only hope. "We will attend to that at the Guard. You should have thought about that before you attacked an innocent human. Maverick, I'll be right back."

The vampire is losing a lot of blood, and that is causing him to feel faint. I force him into a kneeling position as I create a portal to the Guard. I would have liked to stay and help Maverick with the near-dead human, but unfortunately, I have to get Chase to the Guard since he's close to death. I can see the Guard's front doors on the other side of the portal. I grab Chase by the handcuff's chain and force him to stand and walk through. As soon as we cross over and I put my benitoite stone away, we are instantly met by a guardsman working the entrance to the Guard.

"Who do we have here?" Ethan asks.

"Chase. He's a rogue vampire. He attacked a human right in front of us and tore right into her neck. I have to get back and help Maverick with the female human. Chase will need medical attention. Can I leave him for you to take care of for now?" I ask him.

"Yes, of course," he replies as he takes Chase by the same chain I'm holding and drags him toward the large iron doors of the Guard.

I create another portal back to the alleyway we were just in. When I step through, Maverick is no longer applying pressure to the victim's neck.

"She didn't make it," he solemnly says as he takes out his phone to report it to the local authorities.

"Why do they always tear them apart? He could have punctured her neck without doing all that damage. He wanted to kill her." I rest my hand on Maverick's back.

"I know, and they wonder why it's such a strict law about feeding on humans." Maverick sighs.

"I'm going to head back into the bar and remind these bloodsuckers of the laws," I say to Maverick before walking back toward the door we exited earlier.

The other vampires must have known what went down outside because they were no longer in the bar. I did a large circle around all the other humans and found no trace of any vampires. I even checked the bathrooms to make sure they weren't lurking in there. I went back out to Maverick, who was already off the phone.

"It's all done. Are you ready to go to the Guard?" By done, he means that the local police will take care of the body and no doubt call it in as an animal attack like they usually do. There are mountain lions here, and they tend to get a bad rap from covering up assaults from dark ones.

"Yes, I couldn't find any other vampires inside. Hopefully, they take the hint and leave the humans alone for a while," I say as he pulls out his blue benitoite portal stone and creates a portal to the Guard's entrance.

"We can hope." He follows me through to the other side.

"That was fast," Ethan says.

"The victim didn't make it." Maverick crosses his arms over his chest. His hands stained with the innocent woman's blood.

"That's too bad." Ethan opens the large iron doors for us to go through.

Once we're inside the Guard, we take a right into the first door. On the main floor is where all of the offices are, as well as the medical ward. After every incident, we have to fill out a statement of exactly what happened and the outcome. If it's not a crime that warrants a trip to the Guard with a prisoner, we can do the paperwork at home and send it electronically. We are both off shift now, so we decide to get a bite to eat when we finish filling out the statements.

That is another good thing about Graystone, with all the odd shifts the immortal guardians have to work, most stores or restaurants are open twenty-four hours a day. We decide to go to a small place called The Stone Diner. Once we are seated by the cute blonde working the late shift, we look over the menu at all of the options they offer. I decide to go with a steak and French fries while Maverick orders the fried chicken and mashed potatoes.

"Have they told Sierra she's an immortal yet?" Maverick asks once the waitress walks away.

"Nope, and it's starting to get on my nerves."

"I can't imagine being kept in the dark about all of this, then have the world change so drastically." Maverick shakes his head.

"I know, I have to be careful with what I say when I see her, and I hate that." I groan. It is so unfair. She should have known everything by now.

"That must be pretty hard for you."

"It is, but I'm hoping I won't have to hide it for much longer. They told me a year ago that they would tell her by the time she's an adult. She's eighteen now, so she's of transition age," I admit.

"What do you think she will choose?"

"While I don't want to get my hopes up, but if given all the facts, I think she'll choose to go through the transition. The hitch would be losing her best friend, Emma. If anything will sway her decision, that will be it."

"Well, with her being your anima gemelli, I don't think she'll choose the human life." I know he's trying to make me feel better, but I hope he's right.

"Yeah, but I just have this feeling that there's more to her family's story than I've read or seen. Some things just don't make any sense."

"I hear you, but for now, you'll just have to wait. I'm sure it'll all make sense soon. There must be a good reason for immortal guardians of their stature to just go off grid like they did." Maverick sounds reassuring.

"Hopefully I'll find out soon." What a long crappy day this has been. I hate losing humans. Even if I don't know them, I feel like I could've done more to save them.

CHAPTER 5

DANTE

About a week has gone by since I visited Sierra in her dreams. I've been trying to catch her when she's sleeping, but it just hasn't worked out that way. With the uptick in demon sightings as well as unruly dark ones, I've been getting run ragged. I don't know what has gotten into everybody, but it's like most of them are going mad. So far, I've brought in four werewolves, a vampire, and three witches just in the last week. Not to mention a good dozen demons that I've dispatched. Between making portals to here and there, taking the dark ones to the Guard, and all the paperwork that follows, I'm feeling pretty drained.

I'm so glad I have the next two days off. My plan is getting rest and being able to catch Sierra when she's sleeping so we can be together again. I felt bad just dropping that on her and not talking to her for a week. If I had known things would be this hectic, I wouldn't have done it that way. I've managed to see her from time to time in between my missions, but she doesn't and can't know I'm there. What would happen if her parents found out that I was talking to her in her dreams? I kept my word by not interfering for this long, but I can't hold back much longer. My saving grace right now is that they don't know I'm a dreamwalker. As long as Sierra doesn't say anything to them, her parents won't know.

I'm trying to understand why they've chosen to raise her without knowing who she is and what she is capable of. I get that they want to protect her, as do I, but I still haven't found any inkling on this Excalibur guy yet. Maybe he's dead or not creating an army of followers to overthrow the High Council? I'm just a little confused. If he was doing all of that, how come there hasn't been any others coming forward?

I make a portal to my cabin in the woods and take a shower. Next, I eat because I'm starving. I have just been drinking my elixirs and grabbing granola bars or a fast-food meal here and there. That's not ideal for my body, but at least the elixir will keep me at my strongest and most powerful with or without food. I just feel like shit after the fact. My muscles are aching from the lack of good nutrition. I think I fall asleep before I even hit the bed, I'm so exhausted.

After grabbing a snack, I grab my black leather pouch out of the right pocket of my black tactical pants on the floor. This pouch holds the stones that I use when I'm dreamwalking. I can do it without them, but it's harder, and you don't always get who you intend to visit, so it's best to be able to utilize them. I rearrange the pillows on the bed. That way I'm able to somewhat sit up without falling in either direction. I take my amethyst stone in my left hand, which allows me to focus my psychic abilities, and my azurite stone in my other hand, which helps me to channel to the right person.

I sit back and relax with my eyes closed and slowly build the visions that I want in the dream realm. I can choose anywhere or anytime, but with Sierra I always choose my home during daylight hours. This is a dream that I have made many times, so the details come pretty easy. Now I just have to calm myself as much as possible and try to reach out to her. She's sleeping; I can feel her. It's kind of like trying to pull on a rope, slowly the person's consciousness gets closer and closer, and then you can see them cross into your dream. And now I wait for her to come to me. This is always the longest part.

She made fast timing this time around. Before I know it, she's knocking on my door. I rush to the front door and open it as quickly as I can, accidentally spooking her in the process.

"You are real? I'm not going crazy?" she asks with her eyes wide.

"Yes, I'm real. And no, you're not crazy," I say as I wrap my arms around her and hold her tight. The sweet smell of cherry blossoms fills the air. That's what she always smells like, and it's alluring. She wraps her arms around my neck and hugs me back. "I'm sorry, it's been a little while. I didn't mean for it to be that long," I murmur in her ear.

"That's ok. You're here now." She sighs.

I let her go and lead her by the hand into the kitchen and shut the door behind her. She's looking all around, no doubt trying to find clues as to what I had hinted at the last time. She is a very bright young woman. Which I knew, so I took precautions and left out some details from my real home.

"Why is it I can only see you when I'm dreaming?" she asks biting her lower lip.

"I hate to be cryptic, but there is so much you don't know yet, Sierra. I'm trying to give your parents the time to tell you like I promised them I would. I just couldn't hold back any longer. I've been bringing you into my dreams for about a year now, but I had to erase them from your memory each time. But I couldn't erase them anymore. I didn't want to do that to you." Damn, I need to stop talking. I pull out a chair at the small round oak table for her to sit, and then take the seat next to her.

"You've been erasing my memories?" Her eyes widen as she leans away from me. Sierra looks down at her nails and won't make eye contact with me.

"Only memories from the dreams I created, but I didn't have a choice. I'm sorry, I had to see you. I was worried that if I didn't see you in the dream realm, I would break my oath to your parents and see you in the real world." She doesn't understand the bond of an immortal anima gemella yet. When you are away from your soul mate for too long you feel disconnected from the world around you.

"And why did you think I couldn't keep it from my parents then, what changed?" She crosses her arms over her chest and meets my eyes. "Did my parents tell you when they were planning on filling me in on who and what I am?" She sounds a bit irritated.

I can't blame her, though. I couldn't imagine my parents lying to me about who I was for eighteen years and then finding out somebody has messed with your memories.

"No, they didn't. But I'm guessing soon." If she does choose the immortal life, she has a limited window of being able to make the transition successfully.

"Was that you at the mall?" I knew she was inquisitive, but I will have to be careful not to say too much.

"Yes, that was me. I didn't mean to startle you," I say, trying not to smirk. I know she spilled her drink because of it. But of course, Sierra sees my smile.

"Well, that wasn't very nice, you know." She laughs. I could listen to that sound all day.

"I know, but you weren't supposed to see me. I'm usually better about not being spotted."

"So, you do that often?" she asks warily.

"I check in on you from time to time. You will understand why later." I hate having to hide things from her.

"I wish my parents would just stop waiting. You could always tell me, and I can act surprised when they do get around to it," she states like it would be that simple.

"I know it sucks, and I'm sorry, but I can't do that. I gave them my word. I wish it were different. I wish I could be by your side in real life instead of in a dream." I can tell she has so many questions she wants to ask. Maybe I shouldn't have left her memories intact. I decide to change the subject. "How has your week been?"

"Strange to be honest, how about yours?" she says quietly as she brushes a stray lock of brown hair behind her ear.

"Very busy, I've been putting in long days and traveling a lot. That's why I haven't been able to reach you. By the time I get to rest, you're up for the day." That wasn't too bad of an answer.

"Well, I could start taking naps during the day. If it means I get to see you more often," she offers as a solution.

"As tempting as that sounds, I think your parents would start asking questions. My schedule has been all over the place lately, so I couldn't even tell you what time would be good. But I do have the next two days off," I say, hoping she will want to see me.

"So, all I would have to do is go to bed at my normal time?" She raises her delicate eyebrows.

"Yes, and no drinking. It makes it hard for me to find you and connect with you when you drink." Any time somebody is inebriated, they are hard to grasp because their consciousness is like a drunk person swaying here and there.

"Oh, I'm sorry." Her cheeks flush.

"It's okay. I know how it is with Emma. Sometimes that is easier said than done. I don't want you to miss out on spending time with her, though. We will be together soon, so if you do drink and I can't connect with you, that's okay." She doesn't have much time left to just be a teen and have fun with her friends. I guess that's one good thing about the life her parents gave her. She has had more freedoms than most immortals.

SIERRA

I look around his home, trying to find something that could give me an idea of what everybody is hiding from me. All I really see is normal household stuff, like furniture, books, and a few knick knacks sparsely decorating his home. It looks as though he's not big on material items. He must notice me trying to find something because he tries to get me out of here all of a sudden.

"Would you like to take a walk with me?" Dante pushes his chair back.

"Sure." As we both get up from the kitchen table, he reaches for my hand. As soon as our hands touch, I instantly feel the butterflies in my stomach doing somersaults. We walk through the front door, and we step out onto the porch. The view is beautiful. I could definitely picture myself sitting here on this porch watching the sunrise and set.

We walk holding hands for a while without talking. I don't know what to say. I have so many questions I want to ask, but I don't want to push him. I can tell he's trying to hold back, and he's struggling with it. I wonder if Emma was right about me being a royal. That would explain why I needed protection, but why would my parents feel the need to hide it from me? But that wouldn't explain Dante's ability to see me in my dreams, unless he's into that witchcraft and voodoo stuff? All I know is they better tell me soon. This is driving me crazy. I don't know how to feel about him taking my memories away. I'm angry that he didn't trust me to keep it from my parents, but happy about him not being able to stay away.

I take a sideways glance at him and really look at him. He is more gorgeous than he has any right to be. He makes those blue jeans and black t-shirt look really good. With how muscular he is, he must be some sort of bodyguard. Which only makes Emma's theory sound more legitimate. And the way he smells is enough to give me a high. His scent is a mix of sandalwood and cedar. He must sense me staring at him because he turns toward me, and we lock eyes. His emerald-colored eyes are stunning with his dark hair. I could drown in the sea of green.

I can't help it I look at his lips wanting him to kiss me again, and he looks at mine. He bends his head down until our lips meet. And we're kissing slowly like the whole world no longer matters. The only thing that does matter right now is him and I in each other's arms. I don't want him to ever stop kissing me. An asteroid can land right next to us, and I wouldn't care.

My alarm clock jolts me awake. Damn, just when it was getting really good, work had to ruin it. If I can just hit snooze and be back there with him for five more minutes. I would if I knew I could actually go back to sleep. But the way my pulse is right now, I know I wouldn't be able to. So, I decide to just shut off my alarm and get ready for work.

I remake my bed after I get out and grab my clothes for work off of my nightstand to head to the shower. I reach the bathroom and notice my cheeks are flushed. I start the shower while I go to the bathroom so it will be warm by the time I get in. The hot water feels good on my skin, so I stand there and let it rain down on me. I use my shampoo and follow with conditioner then body wash. I do a quick shave of my legs, so I don't have prickly hairs showing with my capris.

That is the nice part about working at Luna's Bookshop, I can pretty much wear what I want and do what I want while working. As long as the work gets done, they don't mind. I do enjoy reading as well, so in between customers and my other duties, I get lost in books. I finish getting ready and head downstairs.

My parents are still sleeping, or at least they're not downstairs. I make myself a quick coffee and grab a chocolate glazed donut from the box on the counter. I sit at the breakfast nook while I eat my donut and look around our kitchen wondering what else my parents have hid from me. I try to think back to anything in my past that could have implied my life was different than I knew. The only thing that I can think of is my parents teaching me to fight and how they insisted on me learning self-defense techniques. Most of my friends' parents didn't make them do that.

Some kids had sports or dance. I had martial arts training. That never really struck me as odd until now. I just thought it was the way both of my parents grew up because they both said they learned when they were young and that it is a skill that will benefit me. I look around at our normal-looking kitchen and try to think of anything else out of the ordinary. Well, time's up. It's almost seven-thirty, and I have to be at work for eight. Depending on traffic, it takes about twenty to twenty-five minutes to get there. That is another skill I learned from my parents, never be late for anything. It is better to be early and have to wait than to be late and have to answer for your tardiness.

My mind wanders the whole way to work. Before I know it, I'm there. I park my truck in the back of the store where the employees park. I finished my coffee on the way here, so I just grab my purse and my water bottle and head inside. I punch into the time clock at the back of the store and head toward Luna's office.

"Hi, Luna," I say.

"Good morning, Sierra." She looks up from a clipboard in her hand.

"Is there anything, in particular, you would like me to work on today?" Sometimes she has specific projects she would like me to focus on.

"Yes, actually there is. A group of kids were in here last night that were reading a bunch of the books and left them scattered all over the place. I didn't get a chance to pick them up yet."

"Okay, I can do that," I tell her.

"Thank you." Luna flashes a warm smile.

"You're welcome," I reply. Luna is a really nice lady. This bookshop was actually her parents' shop when she was a kid, and she took it over when they retired. It has been in this community for decades, and yet still has that small-town feel. The city has gotten built up recently with plenty of big box stores, but the customers still like coming in here over the larger bookstores.

I make my way to the front of the store and put my purse under the counter. I have about thirty minutes before the store opens. I grab the cart from the little office behind the checkout counter and start making my rounds of the many tables. This little cart comes in handy when you have several books to clean up. It has three shelves on it, which makes it easier to sort the books into genres as you collect them. I see what she means; there are books everywhere and from so many genres. One of the books I pick up from the back corner table is about what your dreams mean. I might leave this one on the cart and look at it after.

I never even gave it a thought to see if we had any books about dreamwalkers. I could do some of my own research and maybe find out on my own. I make my rounds and deliver all the books to their designated places just in time for the store opening. It is usually slow on a Saturday morning, so I can probably get quite a bit of research done before the afternoon rush. I settle into a chair close to the front of the store and delve into the book. I have a hard time concentrating on the book, instead I feel a little violated that Dante was able to manipulate my mind without me knowing.

I scan many books and pages throughout the day about dreams and dreamwalkers, and they all have pretty much the same stuff in them. Out of curiosity, I start looking into the books about royalty. We have some in the historical section, so I figure I'll start there. Soon enough, I find out that it's all general information about etiquette and protocols they had to go by and what many of the royal families had accomplished. None of this seems like it would apply to me and my family. I call it a day with research since the store's getting busy anyway.

I think some people come in here just to escape reality. I've seen many people spend an hour or more just sitting at one of the tables reading a book they have no intention of buying. It kind of irritates me because it feels like they're ripping us off. I've mentioned it to Luna before, and she just brushes it off. "As long as they're not taking the book out of the store, I can't fault them for enjoying reading."

The day just drones on and on. I think it's because, for once in my life, I am excited to go to sleep. By the time I get out of work at five thirty my stomach is growling. I have a bagel with cream cheese and a coffee from the coffee shop down the road. I keep wondering what else Dante could have taken from my mind. I have a strong feeling telling me to trust him, but deep down I can't help but question if there was more removed.

CHAPTER 6

DANTE

This past week went way too fast. It was nice being able to spend time with Sierra, even if it was just in dreams. Her parents better tell her soon or I may have to. It's best that she makes the transition sooner rather than later. I hope that's what she chooses. We could still be together if she decides not to go through the transition, but she would always be weaker and have a much shorter lifespan than I. Today is going to be a full day in the city part of Graystone, doing my mandatory yearly physical. They really put your body through the wringer with these tests. But I can't blame them. They need to make sure their guardians are in the best shape to perform their duties.

I just feel a little off today; my mind is elsewhere. I have been trying to get information about Excalibur, with no such luck. I have even been checking in with some informants among the dark ones, and either they really don't know anything, or they're damn good actors. Most dark ones fear the guardians, so most of the time, we can get intel from them. But there are some who think they do not need to obey the rules. Those are the ones you must be careful of. I'm a damn good guardian and I owe most of that to my instincts. My instincts are telling me something terrible is coming. I've had a foreboding feeling these past few days that I can't shake.

I make it through my nearly 12-hour physical with good marks as usual and head back home for the night. I live in Graystone, but it's way off the beaten path away from the city and away from others. It's not that I don't enjoy others' company, but I just enjoy the quiet country life better. My downtime is exactly that, downtime. After having to be hyper-vigilant all the time, it's nice to be able to turn it off. The island of Graystone is protected by magic, so I don't have to worry about any dark ones or demons coming after me. That is, unless they escape from the Guard, which is highly unlikely. They have immortal guardians posted all over the prison ward for that reason. Not that any have successfully escaped, but that doesn't stop them from trying.

It is beautiful here, though. I really think Sierra would be happy in Graystone. Over on the east side, there is Sundial Beach which is a stunning white sand beach that I would love to take her to. She's always had a thing about oceans, beaches, and seashells. There are plenty of little shops over there as well as a small amusement park. Over on my side of the island, it is mostly forested with a few small communities. You could travel all the way around the island in a day by vehicle but you wouldn't be able to make any stops. The island is actually relatively large.

I grew up about an hour from here with my brother and sister, so I feel more comfortable in the woods. They're both on an assignment overseas. Each immortal guardian has zones that they cover, and each zone can have several guardians assigned to it. I'm assigned to the western region of the United States with a focus on Colorado. My brother, Roman, is assigned to Australia, and my sister, Annalise, is assigned to Italy. You have the option of having a house in your zone or making a portal to a home here on the island. I have always chosen to portal back here when I can.

It is amazing to see how different the world is in different parts of it. The traditions and way of life of others have always intrigued me. I think that's why I like to travel on most of my vacations. I try to pick a different country each time, so far, though, I think my favorite place is here. I don't mind staying in other places while I am traveling, but I don't like being around humans for too long. It's not that I don't like them; it's just hard to make much small talk when we are from two totally different worlds. You can run out of safe topics quickly.

Once I get settled and eat dinner, I get set up for a dream with Sierra. It's about one in the morning her time right now, so she should be asleep. I prop myself up in my bed and rest my eyes thinking only of her. Since I gave her the amulet, it has made it easier to find her in a dream, which was a bonus I didn't realize I would get. I finally connect with her, and as soon as she comes into the dream, I'm already waiting for her on the porch.

She automatically comes into my outstretched arms for an embrace. I can't wait for them to tell her so I can have her in my arms for real. All this waiting has been wearing down my nerves lately. I don't know what is taking them so long.

"I've missed you," I say to her instead.

"I missed you too. How has work been?" She gives me one of her dazzling smiles.

"It's been pretty busy lately. How about your work?"

"It's been okay, kind of boring, really. What is it you do for work?" she asks nonchalantly.

"That's classified ma'am." I smirk at her, Sierra will have to try harder to catch me off guard.

"Really?" She shakes her head trying not to laugh.

"Yes."

"Well, it was worth a shot. Is there anything that you can tell me?"

"I can tell you that you're very beautiful." Those words don't even cover it. She has a natural beauty that most women envy. She doesn't have to spend any time putting make-up on, even though she does sometimes. She doesn't need it.

"And you are very handsome, but that's not what I meant, and you know that," she insists.

I can tell the secret I'm holding has been bugging her as well. I didn't think it was going to be this hard. I also didn't think that her parents would wait this long either. We go into the house and sit on the brown leather couch in the living room.

"I'm not sure how long I can hold the dream together tonight. I'm really tired." I hate to say it, but I didn't want her to worry if I suddenly disappear because I fall asleep.

"Why don't you go to sleep then?" She gives my knee a gentle squeeze.

"Because I needed to see you," I state as the obvious answer.

"Needed or wanted?" She playfully pokes me in the side making me tense. I don't like to admit it, but I do have ticklish spots and she knows it.

"Both. Come here you," I say as I pull her in for a kiss. It was just a quick kiss, but even those affect me so deeply. I decide to play it safe and pull her down with me until we are lying side by side on the couch. I wrap her in my arms, and I can feel a lot of my nerves disappearing. Just holding her like this makes the world feel right. She falls asleep with her head on my chest in my arms, and I fall asleep shortly after.

This is how we end most of the dreams lately, cuddling up together until I fall asleep. When I do nod off in reality, I lose the connection in the dream. But most times, I stay sleeping in the real world. It sounds odd to fall asleep in a dream, but I can't think of a better way to fall asleep than with her in my arms. But it is quite the gut punch to wake up and not have her there.

SIERRA

I wish I didn't wake up and realize yet again it was a "dream" and he's not really here. It has been kind of hard to be around my parents lately knowing that they are hiding something important from me. I try not to let on that I'm aware they have secrets from me, but sometimes I just want to yell at them to just tell me already. Between work and Emma, I've managed to stay away as much as possible but still be home on the off chance they will tell me. I have also hung out with the other girls as well. It's hard to believe we're all done school already. Pretty soon, we won't have much time for anything besides our careers.

I have tried to ask my parents questions about what their hiding without coming right out and asking. I've said things like is there any advice you think helped you when you were ready to leave the nest? Or what made you live in Colorado and not elsewhere? They only give me generic answers and the more creative I try to get with the wording just sounds like I'm prying. I know that Dante has strong beliefs about keeping his oath, he's told me a man is only as good as his word.

I've only seen Eric once since my birthday, and it's been kind of awkward around him. He actively tries to avoid me only saying a few words, so it's probably best I avoid him as well. Emma has asked me if I'm still having those dreams, so I have filled her in with some details. She's dumbfounded as to what's going on as well. At least I know she won't say anything to anybody and our secret is safe. This mystery will be even harder to figure out when it's all on me. I don't trust my other friends with any of this, not like they would even believe me anyways. Some days I have a hard time believing it myself and wonder if I am crazy. Maybe I'm having hallucinations.

My parents are both working today, and I think I'm going to try to find something in our house that will tell me something. They must have something here that can help. I stay in bed playing games on my phone until I hear them both leave. I have a few hours free before I'm getting together with Emma. I get out of bed and head downstairs to make myself some coffee. While my coffee is brewing, I decide to start with my dad's office.

I drink my coffee as soon as it cools off enough. I'm skipping breakfast today though my stomach is in knots. I don't think eating would be a good idea at the moment. No doubt worrying what I will or won't find is causing that. My dad works as an accountant so he has an office at home that he sometimes works out of. I don't go in his office often and never without him unless he asks me to grab something. I never had a reason to until now. So when I step in there, I look around with a fresh perspective. I'm going to try to see things that I may have overlooked all these years.

The walls are a light gray with only a few pictures hanging on them. One of the pictures is of all three of us when I was around seven-years old posing with Mickey Mouse in Walt Disney World. The memory of that trip makes me smile. We had such a good time there. Another picture is of Uncle Joe and Aunt Grace in front of their home in Ireland, and the last one is a black and white photo of my dad's parents when they were young. I wish I could have met them. But they died in a car accident before I was born. He doesn't talk about them much. My mom has never mentioned her parents, and I'm not sure why I never asked about them.

The wall behind his large desk has three massive floor-to-ceiling bookcases filled with all kinds of books and trinkets. I never really looked at his books before; I've always assumed that they were just boring old people books. Skimming through all the titles, I find most are about accounting, history, law, and medicine. I try to look through them all without touching anything. There is an old display box with a silver knife in it. I don't remember ever seeing this before. The knife is all silver, but the handle has small gemstones embedded into it. It's pretty cool looking. I wonder where he got that from?

There're a few paperweights and bookends but not anything out of the ordinary. I move onto his desk, which has a lamp with a few neat stacks of files on it. The files have the names of some of the businesses he does books for. I pull open the drawer above where your legs go, but all that's in there are some pens, a tape dispenser, a stapler, an ink pad, and some stamps. The top drawer on the right is filled with blank white reams of computer paper. The next one down has multiple sizes of empty folders and envelopes. The last drawer, however, will not open. I try again, and it still won't budge. I then see that there is a small keyhole next to the handle I hadn't noticed before.

I look around the desk and the other drawers, and there is no key to be found. The four-drawer file cabinet he has is also locked. Which would probably be because he has to be able to assure his companies that their accounting stuff is confidential. I don't know why his desk is locked, though. What does he have in there, and who would he be hiding it from? Most likely that person would be me. But where else would his key be? There's no other logical place to hide it in here.

Since that room didn't turn up anything I could find, I start walking toward my parents' bedroom as a car door slams shut from out front. Crap, I hurry past the front entrance and make my way to the kitchen, hoping I left everything the way it was so they aren't aware I was snooping. I grab my purple coffee mug out of the kitchen sink and start rinsing it just in time for when the door opens.

"Good morning, Sierra," my mom says when she sees me.

"Good morning, Mom." I try not to act like I was doing something wrong.

"I got all the way to my client's house and forgot my tote." She sighs and then disappears into the spare closet to grab her tote. She cleans people's houses for a job, so she brings a tote of all her own cleaners with her.

"It sucks getting old, doesn't it?" I say, chuckling to hide my unease.

"Watch it." She wags her finger at me. "What are you doing today?"

"I'm going over to Emma's in a little while to hang out. Did you need me to do something?" I ask.

"No, just curious, you've been gone a lot lately," she says more like a question.

"I'm just trying to spend as much time with her while I can." Not a lie but not the whole truth either.

She just smiles and says, "Oh, honey, I'm sorry she's leaving."

"I know, me too." I'd rather not talk about it, or I'll probably cry.

"I'll see you later then, okay?" She gives me a quick hug, and she's out the front door again.

I let go of the breath I didn't realize I was holding. That was a close one. After I listen for her car to pull out, I head toward their bedroom. I'm really anxious now. I don't feel right snooping in their stuff but come on, what option have they given me? I stand in the doorway to their bedroom and turn on the light.

Nothing looks out of the ordinary in this pale blue room. But then again, they probably wouldn't leave anything out where I could easily spot it. I start with my mom's nightstand. I open the drawer, and without touching anything, I see some jewelry and some papers, but I don't want to disturb anything, so I just shut the drawer. Next is dad's. He has a few watches in there and a flask? I never really see him drink anything more than a beer once in a while. I decide to open it and smell it, and man, it's definitely some strong liquor of some sort, but I don't know what.

I put the cap back on, replace it the way it was, and shut the drawer. I open the drawers to their bureau, but all I see are clothes, and I don't want to move them and have them notice. Then I open the door to their closet, which consists mainly of hanging clothes, our empty suitcases, and several pairs of mom's shoes. All of our photo albums are on a shelf along with a few boxes, but they are just out of reach.

I grab a chair from the kitchen and step on it to reach the boxes. I take one of them down and open it. It's just a bunch of my old school stuff like pictures I colored when I was little, so I put that one back and grab the next one. This one is slightly bigger but much heavier. I set this one on the chair and open it. It looks like a bunch of memorabilia from our vacations over the years. Maps of different parks, seashells, tickets, and receipts among other things. I put the stuff back exactly the way I found it and put the chair back in the kitchen. I go back to the closet just to double check everything is precisely how my parents left it.

Feeling defeated, I head upstairs to my room and just lay down on my bed to stare up at the ceiling. Am I losing my mind? What could they possibly be hiding from me?

Is Dante real? All of these questions start flooding my brain, and I feel like I can't breathe. I have never had a panic attack before, but I think this is what one would feel like. Out of nowhere, the tears start streaming down my face, and I can't stop. Soon I am crying so hard my throat hurts and my chest feels tight. What the hell is wrong with me? I don't usually cry, even when there are times that I should. After taking several deep breaths I finally manage to slow the waterfall from my eyes.

I need to take a shower. The hot water will help me to calm down. I get under the spray and stand under the hot water for what feels like an hour before I think I am safe to get out without falling apart. I dry off and get dressed. As I'm looking at myself in the mirror, the amulet catches my attention. Besides for showering I hadn't taken it off since my birthday almost three weeks ago when all of this started happening. What if it has a curse on it, and that's what causing all of my crazy emotions? Would that really be less likely of an answer? What would happen if I take it off? Well, I guess I am about to find out if the necklace is the cause of my anxiety.

CHAPTER 7

DANTE

I'm following up on some fairy sightings that were reported to the High Council in the southern part of Colorado. There's a large fairy community that lives in Rio Grande National Forest, and they've been known to cause mischief from time to time. Fairies look similar to humans but have pointed ears and usually have some sort of plant or flower on them, such as a headdress.

I've had to come here before because of the fairies, but it's not usually because they've harmed any humans unlike what this report is saying. The fairies are quite childlike, constantly trying to pull pranks and tricks on anybody they can, but don't be fooled by their playful manner. They're demeanor can change in an instant, and most of them have some sort of magic, such as being able to manipulate plants and just about anything else that grows from this earth. For the most part, they keep to themselves in the forest. But they have kidnapped humans before without leaving witnesses.

I'm glad that it's early afternoon so the sun will be able to light enough of the forest to see our path. The trail that leads to the fairies is not an easy one. There are steep hills and rough terrain. Even an avid hiker would have a hard time on this path. It makes me wonder how normal humans just happen to come across them. After a good hour of walking through a narrow footpath, the dense trees finally start to thin out, and I spot one of the fairies just ahead. He sees me and instantly runs off, no doubt to warn the others of my arrival. Within minutes they have me surrounded as I expected they would. That's why I brought Maverick with me.

Maverick is another immortal guardian like me and has his zone in Colorado as well. We have done several missions together, and he's the closest friend I have. We met at the academy while we were training. In this line of work, you don't typically have a lot of free time, so we don't see each other as often as we would like. It's nice when we can work together though, because I can count on him to have my back. I trust him with my life.

"Mr. Xavier and Maverick, is it? What a pleasure it is to see you both, and what might I ask brings you to our part of the forest?" Alette, the fairy leader, greets me. She is a short, thin woman with pink curly hair and pointed ears. There are two fairy men flanking her, one on each side.

"I wish I could say we are just visiting, but I'm sure you know why we're here Ms. Alette." She only goes by the one name. Most fairies that I have known of don't have a last name.

"Oh, but I don't think I do." She replies with a coy look.

"Ma'am, if you don't mind, can we skip the games? I know you have kidnapped two humans." I am too irritable to play her games today. I can feel that Sierra is having a really hard time. I usually don't feel her emotions as clear as I do now. I thought she was doing okay with all of this. Then all of a sudden, I'm almost swept away by sadness, then anger and confusion, and then nothing.

I think she took off her amulet, which doesn't bode well for me. I hope her parents didn't find out. I need to get this mission over with, so I can go check in on her and make sure she's all right. I can't be distracted while lives are at stake.

"I beg your pardon? We most certainly did not kidnap anybody." She places her hands on her hips.

"So where are they then?" Maverick juts his chin out toward Alette.

Alette cocks her head to the side, "Who is this 'they' you speak of?"

"Maverick, show her," I say, sounding more irritated than I meant to.

"Does this clarify it enough for you?" Maverick holds up his phone with a picture of four fairy men surrounding the two kidnapped teenagers. Apparently, the fairies did not realize there were witnesses—humans who were able to get proof not only of their existence but of them breaking the law.

"Oh, those two, of course, I know where they are. They asked to be escorted into the fairylands, and my men were just abiding by their wishes." She tries to cover up her story.

"You need to release them immediately, or these four men will be brought to the High Council for breaking the law." I plant my feet firmly and cross my arms over my chest.

"There's no need to be so rash. Bring out our guests." Aletta looks to the blonde fairy man standing stiffly next to her. He nods his head and his tall lithe figure disappears behind the leaves of the many bushes.

Within a minute, those same four fairy men photographed bring the "guests" out into the clearing. Streaks of dried tears stain the young adult's cheeks as they glance around them with weary eyes. The skin on their wrists looks raw, as if they'd been bound. "Why are there marks on your guests' wrists?" I ask, challenging her on why she bound the humans.

"To help lead them here, why else?" Alette huffs out a breath. "Are we finished here?"

"Yes, but I do have a message from the High Council. If you take any more humans or harm them in any way, the agreement you have with them will be broken. Do you know what that means?" Maverick's hands are clenching into fists by his side. He's trying to hold himself back.

"Yes, of course, I do," she spits, sounding like a scorned child.

"I don't want to have to come back here. I thought we had a pretty good understanding, you and I?" I meet her gaze. I have dealt with her on many occasions, and not all of the reasons were because the fairies were in the wrong. We've also shielded them from humans and other beings. So, it's in their best interest to abide by the High Council's laws.

"We do. Good day to you both." Alette turns on her heels and stalks toward the thickest part of the forest. The clan of about ten fairies that were hiding amid the trees surrounding us start to slowly dissipate back to whatever tree they came out of.

"It's okay. We're here to help. We'll get you to safety," Maverick tells the frightened young couple. They both nod an answer. That's good enough for me. Single file, I lead the way back down the trail since I know the way better than Maverick, who follows behind the couple to ensure they are protected from both ends.

The walk takes us a while because the humans slow us down so much. On one of the rest breaks they had to take, I give them each a bottle of water and a granola bar I'd stashed in my backpack. They seem to be more afraid of us than they were of the fairies. But if you're to look at us beside the fairies, I can kind of understand why. We're both tall and very muscular guys with various weapons hanging from our backs, belts, and legs. The fairies appear to be cute little creatures with flowers in their hair.

"How did you two find the fairies?" Maverick looks at the young man. "It's not an easy place to get to."

"We heard rumors that there were fairies in the woods, but we didn't venture off the trails on the map the park service hands out, I swear. They came out of nowhere telling us that we were on their lands and that they had to take us as a reminder to other humans to leave them alone." The young man wipes his hand across his sweaty forehead. He looks about sixteen or so.

"What were they going to do to us?" the girl asks. She looks about the same age as the guy.

"I'm not sure, but it is best that you avoid this park for a while, even if you were on the safe trails," I speak softly hoping to ease her fear. I haven't heard the fairies complain about any humans recently, so I'm surprised they kidnapped the couple. There must be more to why the fairies acted out by taking the teenagers.

We make it out of the woods finally, and we lead the teens toward a little silver Subaru in the parking lot. Their friends are waiting by the car with another immortal guardian, Oliver. Oliver has been here the whole time, making sure that word doesn't get out about the fairies and removing any evidence and memories the humans have on the little forest people. This is the least fun part of our duty, making sure the humans stay clueless. Unfortunately, as we have seen too many times in the past, whenever there's something humans don't understand or fear, they try to destroy it.

It would be so much easier on everybody if we could all just get along and share earth the way it is meant to be. Each species seems to want to compete and take over or take out the other.

"Is everything all handled?" I ask Oliver, making sure I'm far enough away that the humans can't overhear.

"Yes, sir, no proof and no knowledge." He nods.

"Good." I turn around and block the two teens we saved from joining their group. "I want you both to look at me and hear me, okay?" I request firmly.

"Okay," they both say in unison, and I know I can alter their thoughts now.

"You have to be careful when you go into the woods. One wrong turn like today can get you lost again. You were dehydrated and exhausted when we found you alone on the forest floor. You were walking around for hours trying to get out of the forest and didn't come across anybody else. Stay out of the woods until the fall." I make sure my mind is telling them the same thing. I always find it amazing how humans are so susceptible and how easy it is to alter their thoughts and memories. It's a lot like what I had to do to Sierra in the dream realm. Sierra was so upset when she found out I did that.

"I know we got lost. It won't happen again," the guy says, and the girl agrees.

Once they drive off, I make a portal for home. It shouldn't take long to type up my report and send it. From there, I can check in on Sierra to see what is going on.

SIERRA

I make it over to Emma's house, and the first thing she says to me is, "Girl, you look like you need a drink." And so, my night of mind-numbing drinking begins. I'm glad her parents are away again. There is no Eric either, so that's a plus. It's just us two, Amanda, and Cynthia tonight. Kayla couldn't make it because she had to work. At least I'm closing the bookstore tomorrow, so I don't have to get up early. My parents don't mind when I stay at Emma's. Not like it should matter; I'm eighteen now and they can't tell me not to.

Emma and I had a long talk earlier before the others showed up, and I told her about my snooping and the breakdown I had this morning. She said she didn't think I was crazy or that it was all in my head, but she did agree that there wasn't any proof that Dante and the amulet really happened either. All I have is a necklace and an overactive imagination. I don't know what to believe anymore. I just want something real to prove to myself I am not losing my mind. God, he felt so real in my dreams, though. And the necklace? Maybe I did find it in a thrift shop. I've always thought all those pendants and stuff were cool. I left it in my underwear drawer so at least I know it's safe and my parents won't find it.

We spend the night drinking and listening to music. We do some not-so-great singing and dancing as well. It's nice just to let loose and not care about anything other than having fun with my friends. I leave for Ireland in a week, and usually, I'm more excited to go, but this summer is just going by so fast. I want to enjoy what little time we have left together.

Maybe when I get settled in Ireland, I can talk about the dreams with Aunt Grace. I know she would keep it to herself, and hell, maybe she's aware of my family's secret. I just realize I never packed any clothes to sleep in. That's okay, though. I can always borrow some of Emma's. We're close to the same size. I am surprised we are all still standing with all the liquor we've drank. We've had more drinks than I can count. I can already tell tomorrow will be a rough one. But I feel good tonight. That's all that matters to me after the day I had. Maybe ditching that necklace for a little while will offer some clarity.

DANTE

After I finish up my paperwork, I check in with Sierra and find her at Emma's. I can see her from the living room window, and she's crying. I wish I can go in there and hold her close to me and tell her everything will be okay. She just has to hold on for a little while longer. I do notice she's not wearing the amulet I gave her. I wonder why? Did I do something wrong?

I create a portal back home so I can get some food and rest. Hopefully, I can catch Sierra while she's sleeping later and find out what's going on. I have a hard time trying to fall asleep, though, because I'm worrying so much about Sierra. But finally, exhaustion wins.

I wake up at about three am Sierra's time and get up to go to the bathroom. On my way I stop by the kitchen and grab a blueberry muffin off the counter along with a bottle of water. Once I've finished with those, I make my way to the bedroom. I put all the pillows on the bed and arrange them where I need them. I grab my black leather pouch out of my pants and retrieve my amethyst and azurite stones. This time I make the setting of the dream my front porch.

I have a hard time connecting with her; her consciousness is very wobbly tonight, which means she's drunk. I keep trying to pull her in, and it's quite the struggle. I finally manage a connection, and I try to hold it for as long as I can.

"What are you doing here?" she says, giggling.

"What do you mean? Don't you want to see me?" I wave for her to sit on the swing.

"I don't know...." She trails off. She's holding onto the rail of the porch refusing to sit.

"What do you mean you don't know?" I slowly walk toward her.

"I don't even know if this is real, if-if you're real," she stammers running her other hand through her hair.

"Baby listen, your drunk. Of course, this is real. I'm right here." I try to make her believe me.

"But are you really? I only see you in my head." She meets my gaze. Her eyes are glossy with unshed tears.

Okay she's kind of right on that one.

I have to give her something without saying too much. "And you know why that is, because of the oath I gave to your dad. Where I'm from your word is worth everything. Where is the necklace that I gave you?" I already know the answer.

"I took it off. It's at home in my dresser. I thought it was cursed. I wasn't crazy until I had that." She looks down at her hands and starts picking at her nails.

"Hey, you're not crazy. I promise you will understand all of this soon." They need to tell her. Their secret is causing more damage than I can imagine.

"I'm not crazy. Says the person in my head." She starts giggling uncontrollably. Quickly her giggles turn into sobs. "What is wrong with me? Why am I like this?" she pleads with me.

The rain came out of nowhere. It starts downpouring in the dream. Large drops of water batter my face and shoulders. I didn't make it rain. I don't know how that is happening. I quickly pull her inside the house out of the weather as the chill of the water soaks into my shirt. The storm must be because of how hard I am having to concentrate to keep her tethered to me. I am losing control of the details in the dream.

"Come here," I say as I pull her in tight, which only makes her cry harder. "Hey baby, it's going to be all right. I'll talk to your parents this week, and if they don't tell you, I will. I never meant to cause you any pain. I'm so sorry." I gently rub her back, which seems to help because her crying slows down a little.

"I'm having a hard time holding on tonight, so If I lose you, I will keep trying." No guarantees I'll get lucky again, though. We stood there, just past the doorway, with our arms around each other. All the while a storm is raging outside. I should have known better than to tell her that her parents were hiding a secret. I was being selfish and couldn't wait any longer. I should have been thinking about what was best for her. The last thing I do before the dream gets ripped away from me was kiss her on the forehead and whisper, "Sierra, I love you."

SIERRA

I wake up to the sound of my alarm on my phone and hit snooze. I must have done that at least three times before I finally got up off the futon. As soon as I stand, I feel light headed. I slowly make my way down the stairs to get a glass of water. I drink it all down and grab a donut out of the bakery box on the table. I am amazed that Emma can eat so many donuts and stay as slim as she does. I swear she eats them every day.

I am feeling a little better but not much. I have to head home to get ready for work anyways. I walk back up the stairs, and everybody is still sleeping, so I grab my clothes and head to the bathroom. I get dressed in the clothes I came here with and leave the pajamas Emma let me borrow in the hamper. I tread lightly toward her front door not wanting to wake anybody and lock it behind me with the spare key Emma gave me. When I reach my truck, I notice that there are flowers in my cupholder. There are three red roses with white baby's breath in a small clear crystal vase.

As I settle into my seat, I pick the vase of flowers up to my nose to smell their sweet scent. One of those small florist shop cards falls from the back. I place the vase back into the cup holder, and I gently open the card, which says, "I am sorry, baby. Everything will be okay soon. I promise, love D-"

Wow okay, I guess either Dante truly is real, or my craziness graduated to hallucinations while awake. I choose to believe the former. I tuck the little card in one of those credit card slots of my wallet for safekeeping. As I sit there for a moment, I think of last night's dream. I can only remember bits of it because of how drunk I was, but I vaguely remember something about him talking to my parents about telling me what they've been hiding.

And then how the dream ended. He told me he loved me, and I didn't even get a chance to say it back. Do I love him? I think I do, I don't know. I have never felt this strongly about anybody else before. When I am not with him, it feels like I am missing a piece of myself. Which is very strange since I have never even been around him while I'm awake. I'm not sure how much longer I can take this secret stuff. I need to know what they are keeping from me. It's not fair. Clearly, it's something important about me.

I head home and am thankful that my parents are both already gone off to work. I make my way to my room and put the vase of flowers on my nightstand. I decide to wear a pair of blue jean capris and a teal-colored t-shirt for work. I bring my clothes with me into my pale-yellow bathroom and noticed how exhausted I look in the mirror. You can tell I had a rough night, so my make-up will have to work overtime to cover up this mess. I don't know which one is worse, the way I feel or the way I look.

After I finish with my shower and put my make-up on, I feel a little better. I still have quite the hangover, though. I grab the amulet from my underwear drawer and stare at it as if this beautiful green gem holds all the answers. I decide to put it back on. I still don't know what to believe, but finding the roses in the truck makes him feel real. I felt naked without the necklace last night. The house seems eerily quiet this morning. That is until a message comes through on my phone.

"Where did you go?" The text from Emma says.

"I had to come home and get ready for work. I didn't want to wake you."

"Okay, will I see you later?"

"I think I need to get actual sleep tonight, LOL. I had fun last night, though!"

"Me too! Are you feeling any better?" she asks.

"I feel hungover, but a little better." I know she meant about Dante but I don't want to talk about that right now.

"Not me, I feel great, ha-ha." Only she could drink like a fish and wake up feeling great. I'm envious.

"I have some stuff to take care of before I leave, so I'll text you later." It's my day to do the dishes and take out the trash, and I would like to get those done before I head out for the day.

"Okay, have fun with that."

"I'll try, you too." And I leave it at that.

The rest of my day is pretty boring, which isn't a bad thing since I have a raging headache. I'm closing up the book shop by myself tonight, which doesn't usually bother me, but tonight I just feel like I'm being watched. With a taser my dad gave me when I got my license in one hand, I lock the doors as quick as I can and head for my truck. My pulse starts racing as footsteps scrape against the sidewalk toward me.

My hand tightens around the taser. It sounds like the footsteps are coming closer. I whip around and aim my taser at—no one. The footsteps have vanished.

I press the unlock button on my truck remote and get in as quickly as I can, and once my door's shut, I press the door lock button. I glance in the backseat to make sure that it's empty. I have seen too many horror movies to know what could be lurking back there if I don't check. I quickly start my engine and take off out of the parking lot as fast as I can. Because I was in such a rush, I forgot to buckle up until I come to the stoplight down the street. What is going on with me lately? I'm not usually this paranoid. Maybe it's all these crazy secrets that's making me jumpy. Dante did mention that he watched over me to keep me safe. Safe from who?

I finally arrive home, and both of my parents are awake sitting at the breakfast nook in our kitchen. They both look as if they saw a ghost when I walk in. My dad is unusually pale.

"Is everything okay?" I dare to ask.

"Yes, everything is fine. How was work?" My dad looks like he is struggling to say those words.

I choose to leave out the part about feeling like I was being chased. "Kind of boring. It was pretty slow in the shop tonight. Dad, are you sure you're okay? You're really pale." I walk toward him and put a hand on his shoulder.

"I'm okay. I just got light-headed, that's all. I've been working a lot lately and not eating like I should." He covers my hand with his own.

"Is there anything I can do?" I ask.

"No sweetheart, thank you, though."

"You're welcome, Dad." I stayed in the kitchen, hoping they'll say more, but they don't. Finally, the awkward silence is too much. "Well, I'm going to head to bed. I have to work in the morning. Good night."

"Good night," they both say as they hug me before I go up the stairs to my bedroom.

That was really weird. I have never seen my dad look like that before. It almost felt like they were going to tell me something, but they decided against it. My parents not trusting me with the information they're hiding is so frustrating. What if I'm adopted? Do they think I'd be angry at them for me not knowing? It wouldn't change how I feel about them if I was adopted.

I get changed into my pajamas and head to bed, hoping to see Dante in my dreams. Unfortunately, I don't see him tonight. Instead, I have a strange nightmare about vampires. No doubt because it felt like I was being chased to my truck earlier. A vampire would be the most logical explanation, not my mind going haywire on me, right?

CHAPTER 8

DANTE

I decided to visit Sierra's parents while she's at work tonight. I have the day off, so I know I won't be pulled away at a moment's notice. I knock on Sierra's front door. My heart is hammering in my chest so hard. I finally got up enough courage to talk to Michael again. I hate to admit it, but even though he is no longer an immortal guardian, he still intimidates me as no other has.

"Hello, Mr. Xavier," he says as he greets me at the door.

"Good afternoon, Mr. Walker. I was hoping to talk to you and Mrs. Walker if you have the time?" I ask politely.

"I figured you would be coming around soon. Come in." He holds the door open for me. After he shuts it, he leads me through the foyer and into the kitchen, where Sophia is already sitting at the table.

"Hello, Mrs. Walker."

"Hello Dante, how have you been?" She smiles as she looks up from the newspaper she was reading and gestures for me to sit.

"I'm doing good, thank you for asking, and you?" I take a seat at the table opposite Sophia. It feels strange to be in Sierra's home.

"I am doing okay." Sophia takes a drink from the glass of water in front of her.

"So, what do we have the honors of your company for this time?" Michael sits beside his wife.

"I was hoping you could tell me when you plan on telling Sierra everything?" I hope that didn't sound rude.

"We're planning on telling her when we get to Ireland. I don't want her to feel like she's alienated and can't talk to anyone else. She's close to Grace, so I hope she'll be more comfortable there." He looks to Sophia who gives him a nod.

I don't want to push my luck, but I can't help but wonder. "If you don't mind me asking, why did you wait so long to tell her?"

"There's a lot in this world you still don't know, Dante. Some of the things that we witnessed while being immortal guardians were unexplainable, and we weren't sure if we wanted our daughter to be a part of that." He avoids my gaze as he rubs at his jaw and glances over at his wife. "But that should be her decision to make, not ours."

"We were hoping to have more answers for her by this time than we do. If anything, it seems like we have more questions," Sophia says.

"Questions about what?" I ask.

"There were a lot of things happening in Graystone when we decided to leave. So much wasn't adding up. And the list of people we could trust kept dwindling," Sophia answers, her brow creasing.

"I did some research on your family after Sierra was born, and I read about your parents and sister, Mr. Walker. I am sorry for your loss." I couldn't imagine losing mine.

"Thank you," he sighs. "I don't want you to think that we have a vendetta against the High Council, but you must tread lightly with anything we tell you."

"Of course."

"We had reason to believe that the High Council was compromised or were glamoured into protecting Excalibur. My parents did not commit suicide. Both of their throats were slashed with no murder weapon in sight. How does one lose the weapon they used to slash their own throat?" He arches a brow. "Add that to the amount of 'untraceable' death threats our family received. We did the right thing by reporting him for treason, but our family has paid dearly."

"I did find that the lack of information in the library on Excalibur was rather odd. I've been trying to do some of my own research but have come up with nothing," I admit.

"The most information that we could find on Excalibur was that he was once the lead Enforcer for the High Council. We found out that information outside the walls of Graystone, though. There was no trace of him in Graystone until we reported him," Sophia says.

"That was what worried us the most. He even carried the mark of the enforcers, but none of the High Council acknowledged his existence. We loved our jobs and home, and it was not an easy decision for us to leave." Michael crosses his arms over his chest. "Unfortunately, we were left with no other choice but to leave if we wanted to stay alive. If he or one of his followers could get into Graystone murder my parents and take my sister, what else is he capable of? And how many others are like him or working with him?" Michael shrugs his shoulders.

"Do you know how many others he asked to join his group of traitors?" I clench my fists under the table.

"No, because nobody else would come forward like we did. Excalibur did say he had others working for him." He twists his lips in distaste.

"We don't mean to make you question your oath, Dante. We just want you to understand the danger our daughter will be facing if she goes there or it's revealed who she is," Sophia says, her eyes clouding with worry. "It's been nearly 150 years since we have left Graystone and about 60 years since we've last heard his name, but that doesn't make the threat any less real. You need to be very careful who you trust." Sophia twirls her short brown hair in her fingers.

"I understand. I will do anything in my power to protect her. You must know that?" I furrow my brow.

"We do, but what if protecting her means she doesn't go through the transition?" Michael asks. "Would you be able to accept that?" He raises his eyebrows as he folds his hands on the wooden table in front of us.

"Well, like you said before, that should be her decision to make. Not ours. If that is what she wants to do, I will still support her. I must tell you, since I am here, though, there has been more dark one activity reported in the last six months than the past two years combined," I warn them.

"I have heard there were more," Sophia says. "Michael, you should tell him what you saw." She looks toward her husband.

"Not many know this, but I have visions kind of like premonitions. Sometimes they happen, sometimes they don't. Sometimes they're clear visuals and other times they're very vague. The one constant in them recently is that Excalibur wants to take Sierra. I'm not sure why or when, but he does take her." Michael's jugular vein is enlarged.

"Shouldn't that be all the more reason that you tell her sooner?" Now I'm starting to get frustrated. "She should know so she can help protect herself." Maybe this is where the bad feeling I've been having is stemming from. I have to try hard not to raise my voice at him.

"It can go both ways. You know how she is. If she finds out that she's an immortal and we hid that from her, she could go looking for answers in the wrong places," Sophia's voice is soft compared to Michael's.

"True, but she's a lot smarter than you give her credit for." I feel like I have to defend why she should know the truth.

"We're leaving in two days, and after we arrive and get settled in Ireland, we plan on telling her everything. She can decide what to do with it from there," Sophia says.

"Thank you for watching over her. I'm sure it hasn't been easy staying away." That sounds like a dismissal to me.

"It hasn't." They don't understand just how hard that has been for me. I don't believe they know I have been seeing her, but I think they suspect something has been going on. We say our goodbyes, and I leave with more questions that need answers. I guess I have my work cut out for me.

I give Maverick a call to see if he can help me find any information on Excalibur. I know I can trust him. We practically grew up together, and he has had my back more times than I can count.

We spent the whole night chasing down possible leads of intel. This Excalibur guy is good at not leaving any loose ends. We didn't find any concrete evidence on anything, but we did confirm he's been building an army of mixed species, pretty much anything on earth besides a human. This intel only confirms what Michael, Sophia and Joe had reported to the High Council about him wanting to overthrow the High Council and gain control over Graystone. Could this be why there has been such an uptick in dark one incidents? The two must be related; it's too much of a coincidence.

The part that puzzles me the most is why Excalibur would want to take Sierra. What is it about her that he needs? Could it be because she hasn't grown up accustomed to the way of life that the High Council has set forward? Or could it be a trap to lure her parents out for revenge? All I know is that I have two days' worth of time before they tell Sierra that she's an immortal and I would like to go back to Sierra's parents with some answers as to where Excalibur is and why Michael's vision shows Excalibur kidnapping Sierra.

SIERRA

Today is a very busy day with saying our goodbyes and finishing up with all of our packing. For a family of three traveling to Ireland for a month once a year since I was five, you would think we would have a system down pact by now. While my mom is doing circles around the house, making sure everything is in line, I sit on our couch in our living room, enjoying the last few moments of being stationary before our trip to the airport.

I really enjoy our yearly family vacation to Ireland to see the only other family that we have who are my Uncle Joe and my Aunt Grace. We live in Colorado Springs, which is beautiful, but nothing is more beautiful than Ireland. I just graduated from high school last month and had my eighteenth birthday. For the last year, I've been trying to figure out where my place is in this world. I definitely want to go college but am unsure of what I'd like to major in. Maybe this month of relaxation and awe-inspiring scenery will help me to know what my destiny is.

I know I should have figured something out by now. I mean, come on, I'm 18, but I feel like I have a purpose in this world but just haven't found the yellow brick road to it yet. My parents still haven't told me what's different about me, and I haven't seen Dante in my dreams the past few days either. I just hope they tell me soon.

I always get emotional leaving my friends, especially Emma. We've been inseparable since the first grade. Even though it's just a month, I promised her I would call her every day. By the time we get back from Ireland, we will only have about a week before she leaves for North Carolina.

"Sierra, are you all ready? Everything is in the car, and your father is waiting outside. You know he's not a patient man." My mom snaps me out of my daze as I realize that she's standing in the entryway with the door wide open, tapping her heeled boot on the floor. She only taps her foot when she's nervous or irritated, possibly both.

"Yeah. I'm as ready as I'll ever be. Let's go." As I walk out the front door, my mom checks all the locks on the door, and when I say all. I mean there are two deadbolts, a lock in the door handle, and a security system. I never understood why my parents are always so paranoid. It's not like we live in a bad city or even a bad state at that. It could always be worse. But maybe if they told me our secret, then it would make sense. Who do we need to be protected from?

I take one last look at our house as I slide into the back seat of our black Tahoe. It's not a huge house by any means, but it's roomy and our home. I will miss my bed. I have a spare room at Uncle Joe's, but nothing compares to sleeping in my own bed.

"Hey, Dad, are you feeling any better?" I ask. He hasn't been feeling well the last few days.

"Yes, I'm fine." He avoids eye contact with me.

I know there's more to it than that; the utter silence confirms as much. Ever since I had my eighteenth birthday, my parents have been acting strange. They seem to worry more about my whereabouts and it feels like they are wary of everything and everybody. I have tried talking to them several times, hoping they will divulge the secret they've been holding, but they never do.

Uncomfortable with the tense silence, I take my phone out and plug my headphones into my ears. I rest my head back and let the music drown out everything. Today is a rock music kind of day, so I decide to start with some *Linkin Park* and then place it on shuffle.

I ride the rest of the way with my eyes closed wanting this day to be over so I can finally see Aunt Grace. We arrive at the airport, so I reluctantly tuck my phone into my black Under Armour hoodie pocket and hop out into the parking garage. As I walk to the back of the Tahoe to grab my bright purple luggage, my dad comes around the other side to grab theirs.

I try to ignore how pale he looks and grab my bag and start heading for the elevators. My parents aren't far behind me. As I'm waiting for them by the large elevators, I wonder what the hell could be going on that could have such an effect on him. My dad never gets sick, like ever. Finally, the elevator doors open with a screech, and we walk in. My mom presses the star button for the main level. Each blinking number above the door seems like it's taking forever. As we arrive at the main level, my dad leads the way through all the crowds, the gates, and the security checks, with such a speed, it seems blurry. Next thing I know, we're in line for boarding.

I always feel nauseous while waiting in line to board the flight. I'm fine once the plane takes off, but this time it feels different. I have a knot in my stomach like something's not quite right, which could be due to my parent's odd behavior or the fact that I know they're hiding something from me. As the line starts moving, the knot grows bigger and bigger, but I just bite down. I've been on many planes, and I shouldn't feel scared about it.

As we find our seats, I slide in first because I always have the window seat. Then my mom goes next, then my dad. A little later, a stewardess comes by and asks if she can get us anything. As we tell her what we would like to drink, her eyes brighten and widen as she eyes my dad. Which isn't unusual; he is a pretty good-looking man, if I do say so myself. His dirty blonde hair and hazel eyes makes many women gravitate toward him. Within five minutes, she's back with our drinks.

"We should be taking off in about ten minutes," she says in a sickly-sweet voice, her gaze lingering again on my dad.

I once again retreat to my phone and send a quick text to Emma.

"Just sat down. I'll text u when I land." Within a minute, my phone vibrates with a new message.

"OK try to sleep I'll ttyl." I put my phone back in my pocket and decide that she's right. I should try to sleep the craziness of today away. I close my eyes as I rest my head back. Out of habit, I reach for my necklace and rub the smooth stone. I only do this when I'm worried, and in some strange way, it's comforting to do. I can feel the plane moving across the runway. I know it's going to make my stomach do a freefall.

Sure enough, it does, but it doesn't last long once the plane levels out. I try to fall sleep again.

My mind won't stop running long enough for me to sleep. I close my eyes and even with music on I just can't shut it off. This is going to be an extremely long day if I have to stay awake the whole time. We only have one stop but the layover is at O'Hare in Chicago. We will be stuck there for about four hours which won't put us arriving in Dublin until almost 6:00 a.m. tomorrow.

To get my mind off of everything that can be causing my dad's "sickness," I picture Dante, lying on a white sand beach beside me. Now that would be the perfect vacation. Just relaxing in the sun with nothing but the sound of the tide coming in. All too soon, though, we land in Chicago, which is kind of a relief because I'm getting pretty hungry. We stop at the Pizza Palooza inside the airport, and each of us orders a few slices of pizza. Pizza is one of my favorites; I could eat this every day and not get tired of it.

The flight is almost eight hours long, plus it's overnight, so hopefully we can all get some well-needed rest. My parents are still very quiet, which is very uncharacteristic for both of them and makes me more anxious. I keep texting back and forth with Emma and Kayla.

Apparently, Eric was nagging Emma about where I was and what I was doing. She said he seemed really upset that I left without saying goodbye to him. I usually always make it a point to see Eric before we leave every summer. But with how he's been lately, I figured he would rather I didn't. Only I would be able to have one hot guy available close by who doesn't want me and have one who does want me only accessible in a dream realm. This summer is just going peachy.

Once we are on the plane, I finally get to my breaking point with the awkwardness coming from my parents. I figure they're trapped here next to me, so maybe I can get them to tell me about my background without them knowing I've been seeing Dante.

"All right, I know Dad isn't really sick. You two have been acting weird lately and even more so the last couple days. What's going on?" I try to ask without sounding like I am accusing them of hiding stuff. Which rightfully so, they are. My parents both look at each other for a moment before answering me.

"We can't really talk about it here, but I promise you once we get settled at Joe's, we'll talk," dad says.

"Are you just saying that?" I cock my head to the side with raised eyebrows.

"No, we will, I swear. There's a lot to discuss." Mom's eyes soften as she gives my hand a gentle squeeze.

"Is it bad?" Of course, it's bad. Otherwise, they wouldn't be acting so weird.

"It's not all bad, but it's too much to discuss in public." My mom points to the back of her seat.

Well, at least I got that out of them. I feel a little relieved that it's out there now, that we need to get on the same page. I retreat back to my music and thoughts of Dante. Too bad I can't dreamwalk and visit him. Finally, my mind quiets down enough to allow me to fall asleep. As I doze off, there's a nagging feeling that there's something I was supposed to do.

I awake with a jolt. The plane feels like it's swaying side to side and bouncing so much that my soda spills all over my lap. I cringe from the cries and shouts from all the other passengers on the plane.

"Mom, Dad, what's happening?" I manage to choke out, wiping the sleep from my eyes.

"Sierra, something hit the plane. I don't know what, but it took part of the left wing off. The plane is going down," my dad says, trying to stay calm.

"We're only a couple of miles from shore. Whatever happens, I want you to promise me you'll swim. With or without us." Tears run down my mom's cheeks.

"Do you think it's him?" she whispers to my father.

"I know it's him."

"Who? Who are you talking about?" I grab the seat in front of me to try to stop myself from hitting my head on the window.

"Just swim. I don't have time to explain. Just get to Grace and Joe, and they'll help you with everything," he orders. It's hard to hear him over all the chaos on the plane.

"I don't want to leave you!" I scream as I start to cry.

"Just remember that we love you, and everything that we did was to protect you," my mom's voice is shaking as she tries to wipe the tears from her eyes as we all struggle to not collide into each other.

"I love you too." Panic starts to set in. This could really be the end to all of us.

"I love you, and we will see you again. Tell Joe that it's him. Be strong, Sierra," my father urges as he looks at me with tears streaming down his face as he unlatches my seat belt. "Remember to swim." I have never once in my life seen my dad cry. Which only makes me panic even more.

The last thing I remember is an explosion of light, then nothing but darkness. No sounds, no sights. This is the end. I'm done. But where's the lighted tunnel everybody talks about? Is that all just some random junk that they tell people when they know they're going to die? Just to follow the light? Maybe it helps those who are left behind, but the ones that go? A total slap in the face.

Because there is no light.

CHAPTER 9

DANTE

I can feel that she is frightened; her emotions are all over the place. She's afraid, she's sad, she's determined. I try to create a portal to get to her as fast as I can. She's in a plane just off the coast of Ireland. It's extremely hard to portal onto something moving, especially at the speed that this plane is going. I'm able to portal to a ship that's close enough to the plane. Luckily when I come through the portal, the humans on the top deck of the ship opposite me are too distracted by the sight of a plane billowing smoke to notice me. I know exactly why she's terrified. Immortals have exceptional night vision. I look up and find a huge man standing on the right wing of the plane; the left wing had already been broken off. I knew at that moment that he must be Excalibur. This is what Michael's visions have been showing, and if he's right, Excalibur will take Sierra.

As my mind tries to come up with some way to get her to safety, I know what I have to do. I have to get to her. So, I create a portal directly to her. Luckily, she has the amulet around her neck again. That is what I aim for.

As I come through the portal on the plane, I accidentally knock into Sierra but I manage to catch her before she hits the aisle's floor. "Sierra! I'll get you out of here safely!"

The man lunges at her parents and in our direction. I quickly step in front of Sierra and block him from getting to her. He raises a fist and aims for my face. I duck, but not fast enough. His knuckles ram into my cheek. Pain explodes inside my head. The plane bucks beneath me and throws me off balance. The other passengers on the plane scurry away from us toward the back of the plane.

We scuffle, and he knocks me aside like I'm nothing. He's far stronger than I imagined. I spring back up with a dagger out and take a swing at him. I don't get him deep, but I do manage to cut his abdomen, which only seems to piss him off even more. Michael crawls over the seats to get at him from behind and hits Excalibur's head and body with his fists. Excalibur turns on his heels and faces Michael. Sophia has a black pen in her hands and jumps over the seat behind Excalibur and slams the pen down hard between the shoulder blade and the base of Excalibur's skull. The enemy lets out a loud growl of agony as he twists toward Sophia.

"Mom!" Sierra is trying to push her way through me to get to them.

"Get her out of here!" Michael yells.

I want to help them but I know what I have to do. What Michael and Sophia want me to do. I turn around with Sierra's face shielded by my chest, my portal stone in my hand and focus all of my strength to create a portal. I have never produced a portal on something moving this fast. The small flicker of light keeps getting jarred around.

I keep trying and trying, but it isn't working. It's almost as if something is blocking me from being able to create one. I have to find a way off this plane, or we'll both die. Since the plane is already breached, I drag Sierra to the emergency exit by the back bathrooms and kick the door open.

"No stop, I have to help them!" she pleads with me, trying to break free of my grasp.

"Sierra, we..." I was interrupted by a bright light that illuminates the interior of the plane. Two more massive men followed by a third slender figure come through the light. I push Sierra behind me and slowly walk backward in the direction of the exit. The colossal men were able to subdue Michael and Sophia. The third man wearing a long black hooded cloak throws a small gold hexagon-shaped box on the floor by Michael and points a long bony finger toward him. I have a hard time seeing what it is through the small opening of Michaels feet. A dust cloud emanates from the box on the floor of the cabin, twisting into a small vortex that envelopes Michael.

"Go now, Dante!" Michael shouts before getting sucked into the contraption.

The warlock has gray eyes the color of smoke and he turns his head toward Sophia next. Knowing there's nothing Sierra and I can do to help I turn her around, so her head is cradled by my chest. She must be in shock because she's not talking or fighting me this time. I pick her up in my arms just as I witness the dust cloud dragging Sophia into the box. I hold my breath and I jump. Once we're outside of the plane, gravity takes hold, and we start falling, faster and faster toward that deep dark water.

"Hold on tight." I cradle her in my arms as we fall feet first into the ocean. The blow of hitting the water is so hard it takes my breath away. Sierra becomes unconscious in my arms. I push with my legs as hard as I can until we break the surface of the water. I keep saying her name, but she doesn't answer. Each time I say her name, the dread in my voice is more and more distinct. We finally make it to shore, and I gently lay her down on the rocky beach, trying to make sure I don't move her around too much.

"Sierra, wake up. It's me, Dante. I'm right here. Please open your eyes," I beg. I don't recognize my own voice. All I can hear are terror and desperation. I have to get her to her uncle's house. He will be able to help me. He has to help me. I can't lose her. I have never been more terrified in my life than at this moment. And I've been through some scary shit. I take my blue benitoite portal stone out of my zippered pocket. With a shaky hand I'm able to create a portal to Joe's house. I pick her up in my arms and I step through it, landing on Joe's front lawn.

SIERRA

"Sierra wake up...open your eyes and look at me."

I can hear the voice. I want to open my eyes or respond in some way, but every time I try to open my eyes, a sharp pain slams into my forehead. When I try to speak, I start choking and coughing.

"Sierra, it's okay, don't talk. I'm going to take you someplace safe, where you can heal. Everything will be fine," a man says as he puts one arm under my back and another arm under my knees and lifts me. I gasp at the unbearable pain that seems to be all over my body. I slump into his arms and rest my pounding head between his shoulder and his neck. I don't have to open my eyes to know that it is Dante carrying me. I can feel it in my heart, I realize as I pass out.

Loud knocking wakes me up, and then I hear the mumbling of voices. My head is pounding fiercely, and my ears are ringing so bad that I can't make out any words. Not long after he sets me down on a couch, I recognize the soft plush of the cushions. This is my aunt's house. How did he know to bring me here?

"Sierra, it's Aunt Grace. If you can hear me, I'm going to start cleaning you up. I need to see if you have any serious injuries. It will hurt, and I'm sorry, but it needs to be done."

"Where's mom and dad?" I shock myself with how scratchy and hoarse my voice is.

"Oh sweetheart, I don't know. They have search teams out looking for everybody. Let's get you cleaned up, and we can talk after, okay?"

"Okay." My body is too tired and hurt to push her for more.

I can hear water running in the background and heavy footsteps pacing back and forth. It must be Uncle Joe. They sound too heavy to be Aunt Grace's. Aunt Grace is all business now, giving me orders not to move. She places a warm wet washcloth on my forehead, and I wince in pain.

"Shhh, it's okay. I'm sorry, sweety. I'm not trying to hurt you," she says in a motherly tone.

She starts dabbing the washcloth on the left side of my face, then the right, pausing in between to rinse the washcloth. My eyes hurt, and it's hard to open them. I manage to open them a little bit and take in my surroundings. I sit up with a wince, using my hands to help me up. Dante and Uncle Joe are talking in the kitchen. But everything is so blurry, and it feels like I have sand in my eyes.

"Michael had many visions of you. You are a very strong immortal guardian, and he knew that you were always watching over her," Uncle Joe says from the kitchen.

"Thank you, sir. But I must ask why doesn't she know the truth?"

"That's a very complicated question, son." He pauses. "He wanted to tell her. He almost did multiple times. He was trying to protect her from Excalibur, and he knew that if he were to go to Graystone with her, there would be a large target on her back. He only wanted what was best for her."

"And what about what she thinks is best for herself?" The pacing stops.

"That's why he wanted to wait until she was old enough to really understand all the risks, not just the glory. I think he was planning on telling her everything here. She has a special connection with Grace, and that would give her an outside person to talk to without breaking the law." Aunt Grace keeps dabbing at my face.

"And what if they don't come back? She only has until the eve of her twentieth birthday to decide." What are they talking about?

"He sent a letter to us to give to her just in case if they weren't able to tell her themselves."

"Do I have your permission to stay here with her and help protect her?" I try to lean toward the voices to hear better.

"On one condition, you will not try to persuade her to go through the transition. Michael was very adamant about that being her choice. And may I remind you she is my niece, and I will stop at nothing to protect her, including from heartbreak."

"I give you my guardian's oath that I will not hurt her."

Immortals? Guardians? Have they all lost their damn minds? Maybe I'm still on the plane dreaming, although I've never felt pain in a dream before.

"I'm going to help you into the shower and get you some new clothes. After that, I have some soup for you to eat," Aunt Grace says. I can't think about food right now, I'm worried about my parents.

The shower feels so good. I didn't realize I was so bloody and dirty until I saw the reddish-brown color swirling down the drain. It's super hard to stand up in the shower. Most of the time, I just lean against the wall. My whole body aches, and all I want to do is sleep. I'm so tired. Aunt Grace had to put stitches at the base of my back. I had a cut across my right side just above my dimple, about three inches long. I also had a cut across my forehead that needed a few stitches.

I especially have a hard time getting dressed. My legs can't do what I want them to do. They are wobbly and weak. Luckily for me, Aunt Grace is right there to help me dress. She slides one arm around my waist, helping me walk to the other couch that I didn't get all gross. As I bend down to sit, a searing pain crosses my lower back. That must be where she put the stitches. It's strange, any normal person would be crying right now. Don't get me wrong, I'm worried about my parents, but I'm just too confused and exhausted to pursue any questioning right now. I feel numb inside.

"I'm going to go grab you something that will help with the pain. I'll be right back, sweetheart." Aunt Grace covers me with a huge red comforter.

Staring straight forward, I nod in acknowledgment. I close my eyes and feel myself nodding away again, and I dream. The plane jolts and we fall. Then a burst of light so bright explodes, making me shield my eyes away from it. As our little family is holding each other tightly, a large burly man steps through the bright light. He has jet-black hair, piercing red eyes, and is eerily calm under the circumstance. His eyes lock onto us.

"Michael, what a pleasure to find you here," the man with the red eyes says in a deep rumbling voice. "And you Sophia, my dear, haven't aged a bit."

"What do you want from us, Excalibur?" my father says in a very clipped tone that I have never heard out of him before.

"Oh, you already know what I want, but will you go willingly is the question? Your daughter here, Sierra, is it? Wouldn't she make an amazing asset to my Revolution?" Excalibur says with a wink in my direction.

"Excalibur, we will go willingly, but you must leave our daughter out of this. She has no part of what's between us," my father says.

"No she doesn't, but she plays a role in what my plan is. You two will go regardless of being willing or not, so will Sierra. I can guarantee you that soon she will see which side to follow. That side will be mine," he bellowed, and I shudder at the thought of what his side is.

Just as he lunges at us, the window beside me shatters, sending glass in all directions. A force knocks me to the other side of the plane, just out of Excalibur's reach. There is somebody in front of me. I struggle to see the face. There's no way I could ever forget that face. It's the same face that has haunted me since my birthday. It's Dante, and he's actually here.

Dante tells me he'll get me to safety. I know he's telling the truth; he would never hurt me. I don't know how I know that or why I just do. He helps me up and stands in front of me. The man my dad calls Excalibur tries to grab at me but Dante blocks him, and they start fighting. Dante is knocked to the ground, but he gets right back up again. Then he pulls a knife out and slashes at him, keeping him away from me.

He wraps his arms around me, and I can feel the heat radiating off him. He holds me tight and tells me I'll be okay. Then all goes black.

I open my eyes and realize that Dante is sitting on the floor in front of the couch. Obviously, those last few hours were not a dream. He is, in fact, here, so that means that my parents are still gone. Did they go with Excalibur, or was that part a dream? I'm still as confused as when I fell asleep.

"Your awake sleeping beauty," Dante says in his husky tone. "How did you sleep?"

"Okay, but I need a drink. We really need to talk. I'm confused. I don't know what's real and what's not," I reply honestly. He sees me struggle to sit up, so he reaches forward and helps me. As soon as his hand touches my back, it radiates heat through my whole body, and I gasp as his beautiful emerald green eyes lock on mine.

He disappears for a bit and comes back with a smile to his lips. He hands me a cup of coffee and a large blue plastic tumbler filled with some green liquid in it he'd retrieved from the kitchen.

"What is this?" I ask as I smell the odd green liquid that looks like blended grass. I should learn not to smell things first; it instantly turned my stomach.

"Your Aunt Grace made it," Dante chuckles. "The green stuff will help you feel better, and the coffee is for you to wake up. We all know how much you need that in the mornings."

Aunt Grace comes into the living room at that time as if sensing I'm awake. "That is my own special recipe. The ingredients have many healing properties and have helped me get over things quickly in the past. Drink up, sweetheart. We have a lot to discuss."

"You're telling me," I mumble as I take a sip of the strange but juice-flavored drink. "Have you heard from mom or dad yet?" I hesitate to ask.

"No, not yet, but I'm sure we will soon," she replies. She clears her throat as a sign that I should down the cup before she begins. I finish the rest of the tumbler; it tastes like fruit punch with a sour kick to it. I set the cup on the small wooden stand next to me and lean back into the couch, picking at my nails, which I usually do when I'm nervous.

"Most of the fairytales that you have heard do have some truth to them. There are such things as witches, vampires, werewolves, and demons among other things but most importantly immortals." Aunt Grace gives me a reassuring smile. Is she really playing a joke on me right now?

Uncle Joe comes around the corner, "My parents, which are your grandparents, were both immortals. Our bloodlines go way back through many generations. We have one of the strongest bloodlines there is. Your father, your mother, and I all grew up in this immortal world, and we embraced it. There are certain laws and rules you must follow as an immortal. One day, a man named Excalibur approached your father, your mother and I. He said he was starting a Revolution and that we should not have to be chained down by the High Council. Together we would be strong enough to overthrow them." He pauses, letting that sink in.

"Of course, your father, your mother and I wanted no part in his revolution. We were immortal guardians of the High Council, and we lived in Graystone. We took our guardian's oath very seriously. We told the High Council about his intentions to take over Graystone, and they didn't even bat an eyelash. They said they were not concerned with one man trying to take them down and that the High Council was well protected. Shortly after we reported him to the High Council, every one of our immediate family started to receive threats from Excalibur for turning him in or not joining him. He said we would pay greatly for being unwise and choosing the wrong path. And pay we did." Uncle Joe looks to his wife.

I'm trying to take in everything that he's saying, but this sounds ridiculous. I sit there silently on the couch waiting for him to continue. Dante is sitting beside me with his hand on my knee.

"We brought all the letters that didn't burn up to the High Council, and still they did nothing, nothing at all. Excalibur is not found in any of the High Council's records. We did not know how old he was or what he was capable of. The only thing that we could find on him was that he was one of the best Enforcers that the Council has had. It's said that his greed for power has changed him from good to evil. He is no longer considered just an immortal. That is why we were so worried. Our little sister, Rosa, went missing the following week after we informed the High Council of Excalibur's treason. We searched and searched everywhere, but there was no trace of her. Three weeks later, we found our parents murdered in our family home, and still, the High Council would not send an army after him. We left Graystone the next day. We did not want to live in Graystone as sitting ducks waiting for him to strike again. We moved from country to country for a while, never staying in one place for more than a few months."

"We are considered deserters by the High Council because we do not fight for them anymore, but what was the point in fighting for them if they would not help their own? We have not been back to Graystone since then, and that was one hundred and forty-five years ago." Uncle Joe takes a drink from the glass of water he is holding. "Your mother told her parents that she was leaving, and they disowned her. They said she was no longer their daughter if she chose to walk away from her duty as an immortal guardian. It hurt your mother pretty bad, but she said she couldn't have meant all that much to them if they could do that so easily. We have not heard the name Excalibur in about forty years, so we thought we were safe. Eventually, we settled down in Colorado Springs under the last name of Wilson."

"Wait, what do you mean the last name of Wilson? Is that not our last name?"

"Our real last name is Walker. Unfortunately to be able to hide among the humans without Excalibur or the High Council finding us, we had to take on several aliases."

"Oh, that makes sense now." That is all I can say. I rub my forehead, feeling my headache getting worse.

"When you were about a year old, I came here to Ireland on a vacation and met Grace. I never had the typical immortal soul mate like you two do, but for me I don't need a magical bond to tell me who my soul mate is." Uncle Joe looks lovingly at Aunt Grace.

"What is the High Council?" I try to recall everything he said. My head still feels fuzzy.

"Think of it kind of like a courthouse. There are six council members and one Master Council, who enforce all the laws of immortals and dark ones. They are also the ones that decide punishment for laws that have been broken. The main two laws that we have are not letting a human being know what you are and only using your powers for good, not evil. The High Council is located in the heart of Graystone, which you can't find on any map. Your only way into Graystone is to create a portal there. There are magical wards around the island, that ensures that only witches, warlocks, and immortals who have pledged an allegiance can cross. Our duty as an immortal guardian is to protect the human beings from rogue vampires, werewolves, witches, and even demons. If any bring harm to the human population, we detain them and bring them to the Guard for punishment."

"What would Excalibur want from my parents if they left all this behind?"

"My guess since he didn't kill them right off, he plans on using them to take down the High Council." Uncle Joe runs a hand through his short hair.

"Then how can we stop him and get them back?"

"I'm working on that part." Uncle Joe glances at Dante.

"You were saying the choice is mine to make. How do I decide?"

"If you want to embrace this life, you must go through the transition by your twentieth birthday. That is not a decision you make on a whim, though. The transition is very painful and is a risky process, also permanent. You would be forced to leave this human life behind. I'm sure this is overwhelming, so you should take some time to think about all of it. You have a letter from your parents, which will better explain why they did what they did, but I will be here to answer any questions that you have." Uncle Joe reaches up and rubs my shoulder.

"Okay." I don't know what else to say. I can't believe that I never knew about any of this. The whole thing is a lot to take in.

"I may not be an immortal or have any children of my own, but I do have some knowledge on this subject. I always thought of you as my daughter. If you need anything, don't hesitate to ask." Aunt Grace gets up off the couch.

"Thank you so much. I don't know what I would do without you guys right now. And I have always thought of you as a second mother." Aunt Grace smiles at me and gives me a hug. She then disappears into the kitchen.

"I'll go grab the letter your parents wrote and give you some time to read and think about what's in it," Uncle Joe says also giving me a hug.

JOE

Right after I told Sierra about our twisted past Grace and I retreat to our bedroom for a quiet moment. I didn't expect to be the one who had to tell Sierra. I hope I did it the way Michael and Sophia would want me to.

"I think she took it rather well." I shut the bedroom door behind me. I want to give Sierra some time to process all of the information that I just gave her.

"I think so too, but it will probably take a few days to sink in. What are we going to do about Sophia and Michael?" Grace sits down on the edge of our bed.

"I don't know where to start." I frown.

"How about seeking the guidance of the High Council? I know you don't want to, but what other options do we have?" Grace asks gently.

I rub my hands through my hair and just let my arms fall back to my sides defeated. "That seems like the only logical conclusion right now. Although I want to warn you that the High Council may seek punishment on me for abandoning my oath as a guardian." I take a seat next to my wife on the bed.

"Even though you're justified in your decision to leave?" Grace puts her hands on her hips.

"I grew up on a set of values to protect the humans from evil, which I still believe is necessary. But at what cost is the freedom of humans when immortal guardians are just a number with no freedom to choose the life they want to live?" Now that I say that out loud, it kind of sounds like Excalibur's madness. I sigh.

"What do you think Sierra will choose?" Grace leans her head on my shoulder.

"Dante is a full immortal guardian, one of the best I've been told in a very long time. If it came down to choosing her current life or a life with him, she would choose him. An immortal soul mate is not only an emotional bond with another person, but it is physical as well. It causes one pain to be away from their anima gemella. And after a while, immortals have been known to go insane from the loss of a soul mate. I knew if I were in her shoes, I would choose whichever life had you." I cup her cheek and look into her eyes.

I stare at absolutely nothing on the floor while contemplating my options. I could try to go after Excalibur, but on second thought, that would be a suicide mission. Not only have I been out of the game for a long time, but also even at my strongest, I would be no match for him. Who knows how many immortals or other creatures he has already converted to his Revolution? I might as well walk in there blindfolded with my hands tied around my back for all the good it would do. Helpless is not something I handle well. As much as I want to be the knight in shining armor rushing in and saving Sierra's parents, who would be here for Grace and Sierra if I don't come back? From what Michael told me of his visions, Excalibur wants to kidnap Sierra.

I break out of my trance as Grace wraps her arms around me. "I love you and will support you on whichever decision you choose, but you must choose soon."

"I know you will, and I love you too."

CHAPTER 10

SIERRA

As I sit on the bed in my guest room at Uncle Joe's, I feel numb. I have the letter sitting on the bed in front of me, but I can't gain the courage to open it. So instead, I just sit there and stare at it, wishing the last 24 hours can be erased. Dante told me he would give me some time alone, but he'll be right out in the hall if I need him. All the horror movies I've seen flash before my eyes. How could I have been so oblivious? Pushing all other thoughts aside, I pick up the envelope on the bed beside me, wondering how one normal-looking envelope could hold all of the answers to this crazy world I just fell face-first into.

On the envelope, my name was written in my mother's elegant scroll. As I see her beautiful handwriting, the tears start to well in my eyes. I turn the envelope over and hold my breath as I undo the small metal clasp on the back. I tip the envelope upside down to let the folded papers inside slide out in front of me. I grab the one that's on top first and open it up.

"Sierra,

If you are reading this, then something bad has happened to your father and I. As hard as this is for you, you need to stay strong. You are a courageous, and kindhearted woman. Always remember that. The reason for this letter is that there are some things about our family that we haven't told you to protect you. We wanted to wait until you were mature enough to know who you really are. Your name is Sierra Rose Walker, and you are what is called an immortal. Your father and I are full immortals as well as Uncle Joe. Most of the scary things in fairytales are true, and we're sorry we hid this from you. If you can imagine it, it's out there. Your father and I are descendants of other immortals, and our bloodline is very strong. Which means if you chose to embrace this life, you could be a very powerful immortal guardian. I met your father while training in Graystone, which is a land for only immortals and witches or warlocks. That is the immortal headquarters where all young immortals train to be guardians or learn other duties chosen for them. Immortal guardians protect humans from werewolves, vampires, and other types of evil in the world. Uncle Joe can explain the reasons why we left our duties behind. We are sorry if you have to suffer an ill will because of our leaving. We waited a long time before we decided to have a child. We wanted to make sure that you would be safe. I wish that your father and I could have been there to help you through all this and explain it to you ourselves. You should seek out Uncle Joe. He is very knowledgeable and can help you. In this envelope you will find a small key fob that will open a secret room in your father's office behind the bookcase. In this room, you will find immortal elixirs, a map of Graystone, many weapons as well as some very important paperwork. There is also the Immortal Code book, which is a manual if you choose to be a full immortal. You can find a lot of answers in there as well. There is also a list of contacts that you can seek out to help you with the transition. We have enclosed a list of accounts we have set up to help secure your future. There are also several of my old guardian-issued black uniforms that should fit you in there. I'm sure that you will have many questions, and Uncle Joe is fully prepared to help you in our absence. Although you are still an immortal without going through the transition, you will not have all the benefits of being a full immortal. You may live longer than most humans as well as heal faster, but that will be about it. We love you very much and will be proud of you, whichever way you choose. Remember sweetheart, you're a shooting star, so aim for that galaxy. We hope to see you soon.

With love,

Mom and Dad"

I sit on the bed for a few more minutes trying to take it all in. When Dante had told me that my family had a secret, I never would have imagined anything like this. I guess all the clues kind of make sense now. I carefully get up off the bed and go to the door to open it, and as soon as I do, Dante is there. My gorgeous savior who has always been there, I just didn't know it. He quickly gets up off the hardwood floor. He opens his arms, and I immediately go into them. As he wraps his muscular arms around me, I feel like I could stay in the safety of his embrace forever. That nothing can hurt me when I'm there.

"Are you okay?" He gently rubs my back.

"I think so. I'm just worried about my parents," I reply honestly.

"I know, baby, I am too. We'll figure this out. We'll get them back." He sounds very confident.

We go back out to the living room where Uncle Joe and Aunt Grace are having a quiet conversation. They both look up at me and try to give me a reassuring smile.

"Have you heard from my parents yet?"

"No, and to be completely truthful, I don't think that we will," Uncle Joe says.

"I think we should inform the High Council now if they don't know already. The only silver lining to this would be that he broke the law by harming or possibly killing humans, so now they have to pursue him. What are the casualties so far?" Dante asks as he glances at the TV with the news on.

"The local authorities are combing through the wreckage as we speak. The pilot was able to level out the plane and slow it down before it crashed into the ocean, so hopefully some were able to get out. But crashing into the sea will make it harder to find all the victims. The last I saw, it was up to 45 confirmed dead, but they are not expecting many survivors, if any. The news reports are saying there were close to 300 people on board," Uncle Joe says somberly. It dawned on me that my friends back home will think I was on it when it went down.

"I have to tell Emma I'm okay." I start to reach for my phone, realizing that I must've lost it on the plane.

"We have to be careful because we don't want to raise any questions as to how you managed to get off that plane while others didn't." Uncle Joe rubs his eyes.

"So, I'm just supposed to let everyone think I'm dead?" I ring my hands out to try to release some of the tension building inside me.

"We can get word to Emma, but that's it," Uncle Joe says right before the TV broadcasts more news.

"We are just getting word that there are some survivors who managed to get off the plane before it crashed into the ocean. The Maritime Search and Rescue team is pulling people out of the water as we speak. The pilot was able to decrease the speed of the plane and take it out of a nosedive. The surviving victims are reporting that a young man was able to get the emergency exit door open and urged people to jump into the water when they got closer. Between the pilot minimizing the force of the crash and the fast acting of the other man, they may have been able to reduce the amount of casualties."

Dante looks relieved he was able to save some of the others as well. We all stare at the TV without talking, waiting to see what else the newscaster will say. "The identity of the young man is not known at this time, as well as if he is among the survivors or the deceased. That is all we have for now. Stay tuned for updates as we get them. This is a breaking news story and will be updated as soon as we have more information."

"Did anybody see you create a portal?" Uncle Joe asks Dante.

"I didn't see anybody around on the beach when I did. But to be honest I didn't really look. I'm going to go call upon the High Council so they can assist," Dante replies as he steps out the back door onto the porch.

DANTE

Once outside in the backyard, I make the call to the High Council. I need a moment to gather my thoughts and decide the best wording to explain my decision and what is going on. I already know to be wary of trusting others. I will be as honest as I can be without letting them in on me knowing the whole story of Excalibur. After the third ring, someone picks up.

"Gabriel, cleric to the High Council speaking. How may I assist you?" he asks in his professional manner.

"Hello Gabriel, this is Dante Xavier. I have to inform the High Council of an incident I was involved in."

"What is the nature of the incident?"

"I was on the plane that went down off the coast of Ireland. It was another immortal who caused it."

"I see, hold on while I check to see if they are available." He puts me on hold and the line goes silent. I'm pacing in the recently mowed grass. I'm glad the slight breeze is able to come through the wood line, it's warm and muggy out today.

He comes back a minute later. "The High Council will speak to you now. I will transfer your call to the conference room."

"Thank you."

"You're welcome," he replies as the line goes silent again.

"This is Ryker, Master Council of the High Council speaking. You have all seven members present," he says in his deep, authoritative voice. "Start from the beginning."

I tell them every detail that I can recall, hoping that this will force their hand to act. With Excalibur being this brazen about an attack there's no telling what he is planning next.

"Thank you for informing us of the situation, and we will discuss our options and let you know if we will require anything more from you."

"Thank you, council members," I say right before the line goes dead. Hopefully, they can help. If not, I really have to work on a plan to get them back. I turn toward the house, and Joe meets me at the door as I open it.

"Can I have a minute?"

"Yes, of course."

He steps outside and shuts the door behind him. "How did it go with the High Council?"

"It went okay, I think. I didn't tell them anything you or Michael have told me. I figure it is best not to."

"I agree, no telling what they would do with that information," he says.

"The way I framed the wording didn't give them an option not to act. So, if they don't do anything after he killed numerous humans, I think it would cause an uproar among many immortals."

"Let's hope it doesn't come to that. I'm waiting for Excalibur to use Michael and Sophia as leverage or bait." He sounds exhausted.

I look him in the eye. "Well, I will help with whatever I can, but Sierra has to be my priority." He has to know where I stand.

"I wouldn't expect anything less. Let's go back in, and hopefully, we'll hear something soon." Joe heads toward the door.

"I can't imagine how hard all of this is for Sierra." Even though she seems to be taking it better than I imagined. Although, she may be in shock after the day's events.

"Neither can I, but I know my brother made the best decision when it came to her welfare. She's strong, she will be okay." He tries to reassure me.

"I know she is." She will get through this. She has to.

Chapter 11

SIERRA

The day drags on with no word from my parents. I'm worried sick about them, but Dante and Uncle Joe told me to try not to fret too much because of the amount of training that my parents have gone through. I still can't believe everything that transpired today. My parents were going to tell me themselves when we got settled here. Would it have ended differently if I had known? Could I have helped them instead of being somebody that needed saving? All of these questions keep flowing through my mind like a raging river that I can't hold back.

Dante had a follow-up call with the High Council, and they informed him that they are opening a formal investigation. They will be sending a team of investigators and specialists to help out and make sure nobody suspects the involvement of non-humans. Wow, that sounds weird to say. I was able to make a quick phone call to Emma on one of Uncle Joe's burner phones. I simply told her that I was okay but that I couldn't tell her anymore.

I also told her I lost my phone but would be in touch soon and not to let anybody know that I made it yet. That was Uncle Joe's idea which is kind of messed up, but I get it. Excalibur was after me as well, and he may not know I'm alive. The only ones who do are the people in this house and the High Council. If Excalibur knows for sure I am alive, we know it came from them.

Even with all of this going on, Uncle Joe said Dante could not sleep in my room with me. Fine, I'll just have to sleep out on the couch with him instead. I feel safe when I'm with him. I know he'll do everything in his power to keep me safe. He proved that today. I don't know what I would do if he died trying to save me from Excalibur. I shudder at the thought of that man, or whatever he is.

He's obviously more than just an immortal from what Uncle Joe and Dante have told me about immortals. But I still don't get why he would want to take me. It's not right him taking my parents, but in his own twisted way, that was probably revenge for turning him in. But what have I done to him? Prior to today, I had no idea about any of this hidden realm on Earth.

My wounds are already starting to feel better, thanks to Aunt Grace's concoction. My head still really hurts, though. I think that could be related to the amount of craziness that has been slammed into my brain these last few days. I had asked them all a bunch of questions about immortals and what the transition would look like. They answered every question I threw at them, no matter how dumb the inquiry.

If I choose to become an immortal guardian like Dante, I would have to leave my life behind. That means all my friends back home could not know what I am or what I do. I could still have them in my life for a little while, but they'll eventually notice that I don't age anywhere near the amount I should. Then at that point, I would have to do something. And that is what's holding me back from wanting to go through the transition.

I can't imagine my life without them, especially Emma, but I can't imagine my life without Dante either. I like the idea of having a higher purpose, such as protecting others, but the cost I would have to pay is what scares me the most. Emma has been my constant throughout my whole life. We've been best friends since the first grade, and I can't really remember life without her. She's like a sister to me. But when I am with Dante, I feel like I'm where I belong. I don't know what I should do, and I wish I could talk to my mom right now. She has always been good at weighing the pros and cons of any situation. I'm not mad at them for not telling me. They had their reasons. I just wish I could've helped. If I had known, surely I could've done something.

Dante and I are lying down together on the couch in the living room. Uncle Joe and Aunt Grace have gone to their bedroom for the night. I know he's not sleeping by the way he's breathing, but the silence isn't awkward. It's kind of nice to just lay there and not have to engage in any conversation. He gets what I need without me having to ask. When I asked him what he thinks I should do, he told me to do what feels right to me.

I'm just worried I'll make the wrong decision whichever way I go. Once I am past twenty, I can still go through the transition, but the likelihood of me surviving it drops drastically. I wish I could tell Emma about this, but I can't. The number one rule is to not be known as anything but human to the humans minus extenuating circumstances.

Finally, fatigue wins the battle, and I fall asleep on Dante's chest listening to his heartbeat. For once, I don't dream about anything, I just sleep. My body and my mind are too exhausted to come up with a dream.

DANTE

A few days have gone by since the attack on the plane, and still there is no word on Michael and Sophia. I have already given a written statement to Grady, who is the lead investigator on Excalibur's case. Sierra has been very quiet the last few days. No doubt she's overwhelmed by everything. I wish I could take it all away and carry it for her, but unfortunately, I can't. This is something she must endure herself, but I can be there to support her. Excalibur has not tried to come for her so that is a good thing, but the High Council still haven't found him either.

I secretly wonder if the High Council is even looking for him. I hate to feel this way, but I can't help it after everything I have learned about them recently. They are causing me to doubt the Guardian's Oath to always do what is right for the greater good. I don't see how that oath applied to them when they refused to back Michael, Sophia and Joe. I would think that the greater good for all would be to take Excalibur out of the equation.

I don't like admitting it, but I don't know what we're up against, and that thought scares me. Excalibur is not just an immortal. I had heard whispers among the dark ones that he had transformed himself into something more, but what? It could be demon magic; I've heard of warlocks and witches bonding with demons before. The demons almost always win when they possess somebody. Maybe he's stronger and more able to control the demon than others. Either way, we need to know what he is so we can prepare.

After talking to Joe, I found out that Sophia has supernatural swordsmanship as an ability which could explain why she was such a legendary immortal guardian. Joe has shapeshifting abilities and Michael, well, he'd admitted to having premonitions before he disappeared. All immortals are not granted extra gifts, so to have that many in a family is rare. The three of them together would make an unbeatable team. It's no wonder Excalibur would want them as allies. It is an unwritten law that our extra abilities or skills can't be documented anywhere. That way any potential enemies would not be able to have the upper hand. Did Excalibur know about their abilities and that's the reason he wanted them as part of his revolution from the start? I still don't know how Sierra fits into all of this. Maybe Excalibur was hoping to use Sierra as leverage to force her parents to help him.

I had told Joe that I was a dreamwalker and he simply said, "Is that how you got around Michael asking you to stay away?"

"Well to be fair, I erased her memories every time up until she turned eighteen." I still feel guilty about doing that to her.

"You know he always thought you were around, but never found out how. He had a feeling you were seeing her. I guess that explains it," Joe said, chuckling.

I hope Michael and Sophia take it as good as Joe did. I never meant any harm. I just couldn't stay away. How can they fault me for loving their daughter? I hope I get the chance to explain myself. I don't want Sierra to lose them both because of Excalibur.

The total casualties from the plane are now two hundred thirty-nine humans. Twenty-four were able to save themselves by jumping out of the plane and staying afloat until rescue boats arrived or by swimming to shore. I would hate to think if I hadn't intervened and the pilot wasn't able to straighten the landing how high the number of deaths would be.

I requested to take a short leave during this time so I can focus on Sierra and her family. I know that the High Council is not happy about it but they don't have grounds to deny it. Besides, it's not like they even asked me to help with the investigation.

I'm sitting on a patio chair on the back lawn watching the small birds at the bird feeder while Sierra is in the shower. It is peaceful here, I can see why Joe loves it. His house sits back from the road and the lawn is surrounded by trees. He has neighbors but they can't see through the thick brush that lines the property.

"Can you take me to Graystone? I want to go through the transition," Sierra asks me, breaking me out of my trance.

"What?" I think I heard her wrong.

"I want to go through the transition. Can you take me to Graystone?" She rephrased the question.

"Are you sure you know what you are asking?" I search her face.

"Yes, I do. And I want to help. I can't just sit here and do nothing." She flails her arms out.

"Is that why you want to do it?"

"It's not the only reason, but it's the reason I want to do it right now." She sounds determined.

"I just want to make sure you know what you are asking." The neighbor's dog is barking which puts me on edge. I glance around the property.

"I have thought about it constantly the past few days and this is what I want. Don't you want me to?" Her brow dips. I get off the chair and wrap my arms around her.

"What I want is for you to be happy and be able to live with whichever decision you make." As much as I want her to go through the transition, it has to be her decision. That much I do agree with her family on.

"Well, I want to do it." She looks up to meet my gaze and holds it.

"Okay, we'll go talk to Joe and let him know." I follow her to the back deck where Joe and Grace were preparing the grill to make dinner.

"Uncle Joe, Aunt Grace I have decided that I want to go through the transition." She catches them both by surprise.

"Are you sure?" Joe glances toward me and away from the grill.

"Yes, I am. And I would like to do it now." She makes strong eye contact with Joe.

"You do realize it's not a fast or easy process, right?" Joe puts the tongs on the side of the grill and raises his eyebrows at Sierra.

"Yes, I know you and Dante have informed me of everything including all the risks. It's my decision to make and this is what I want to do." She holds her chin high.

"Okay if that is truly what you want, we can head to Graystone first thing in the morning." Joe let out a deep breath.

"Yes, it is. And thank you, but I don't want you to go if you will get in trouble," she says to her uncle.

"I'll be fine, now that there's an investigation going on more immortals are aware of Excalibur and what he's capable of. They may be able to justify why we left like we did."

I really hope he's right. The last thing Sierra needs is to lose one more family member because of Excalibur. We head into the house and she leads me to her little bedroom in the back of the house. She shuts the door behind us.

"I never did say thank you for saving me, did I?" she asks me.

"Yes, you did that morning."

"Oh, I don't remember. But I wanted to tell you again anyway. Thank you for always being there even if I didn't know you were there. I can't imagine what could've happened if you didn't get to the plane when you did." Her eyes are tearing up.

"Your welcome baby. I know everything is kind of crazy right now but we will get through this. I can't imagine you not being in my life. You are the reason I remember to breathe and the reason I get up every morning ready to face this scary world we live in," I say to her, feeling vulnerable. I was terrified of losing her, and the threat is still there.

"I love you," she says.

Who knew those three small words combined could have such an affect on me? I wasn't sure if she heard me last week when I told her that I loved her.

"I love you Sierra, more than anything in this world." I bend down to kiss her and she meets me halfway. For several minutes we kiss, but as hard as it is, I pull away. "Slow down there baby, I don't know what Joe will do to me if he finds me smooching his niece like this," I say, chuckling.

"He'll get over it." She brushes her lips against mine. I don't want her to stop but if Joe were to see this, I think I may be a dead man. They're not innocent kisses she's giving me. These are the type that makes your knees go weak and make everything else disappear.

SIERRA

I didn't want to stop kissing him. The butterflies he gives me every time we touch are magnified when his lips are on mine. Nothing else matters in this moment but us. He pulls away again, and the way he looks at me makes me think he doesn't want to stop either. He takes a step back.

"Are you really scared of Uncle Joe after everything you've gone up against?" I ask him, not even trying to hide my laughter.

"He's a scary dude!"

I love how he can make me laugh even in times like this. "Well, we better get out there before he wonders what we are doing then."

"Your right, I don't want to be on the receiving end of his questioning." We walk out of the bedroom and right into Uncle Joe.

"On the receiving end of who's questioning?" he asks, no doubt overhearing everything we just said.

"Nobody's, we were just joking around." I try to spare Dante from the daggers Uncle Joe's eyes are throwing at him. Yup, he definitely heard our conversation and decided to play along.

"Are you doing things to my niece you shouldn't be doing under my roof?" He looks to Dante with his eyebrows raised.

"I just kissed her, that's all, I swear." He holds his hands up, defending himself.

"It's okay. I'm just messing with you. No more than kissing, though, got it? And the door stays open."

"Really Uncle Joe, you do realize I am an adult, right?"

"Just barely an adult. I can't help it that you're still a little girl in my eyes," he admits.

"A little girl who can go into town and get a hotel room. Just remember that with your old-fashioned rules Uncle Joe, I don't have to stay here." I make him really think about that.

"You're right, I'm sorry. I just can't believe how grown-up you are." He looks at me wistfully.

"I know," I say, and we leave it at that. Dante looks pretty relieved that conversion is over. I can't say I blame him. Now that I think about it, my uncle can be pretty scary.

Dante helps me set the table for dinner. Aunt Grace is making coleslaw to go with our steaks that Uncle Joe put on the grill. I'm lucky to have them as an aunt and uncle. I don't know what I would have done without them. They have taken such good care of me these last few days.

I hope he doesn't get in trouble with the High Council because of me. From the sounds of it, they're pretty strict on law-breaking, even if it was justified. With everything going on right now with Excalibur, that should solidify the reasoning behind their leaving.

I believe I made the right decision. I know it's going to hurt me tremendously leaving my friends, but I have a while before that happens. I think becoming an immortal guardian is what I was born to do. That is my higher purpose. It seems coming to Ireland did reveal my destiny.

We eat our dinner quietly, all of us in our own little worlds. I worry what tomorrow will bring. I really hope the High Council will allow me to go through the transition to become a full immortal. Dante already warned me that the training I have to go through would be grueling and feel endless. But that is what makes the immortal guardians an unbreakable force. I'm excited at the opportunity but also terrified that I will fail. I want to help rescue my parents, and this will be the best way I can help, and maybe, just maybe, I can help clear their names in the process. And to think Emma and I were joking that I was a princess, how wrong were we. God, I miss her.

The rest of the night goes rather smooth. We talk quite a bit and just enjoy each other's company. When the time comes to go to sleep, though, I can't. Instead, I try to mentally prepare myself for tomorrow. There is a whole big ritual that I will have to go through to become a full immortal. Joe said the transition is the most physically painful thing he has ever been through, but once you wake up after the coma like sleep your body puts you in, there is no lingering pain. So, if I can just make it through that, I will be okay. I can't believe this is happening, and my parents aren't even here to see it. I hope they will be happy with my choice. I miss them both so much.

Chapter 12

DANTE

I am worried for Sierra. I don't think anything can prepare her for what a transition will be like. At least for Joe and I, we grew up in Graystone so we witnessed others going through it prior to ourselves. I know she's strong and capable and can do it. I just don't want to see her in that much pain. Not to mention the slight chance that she won't survive it. I don't think I could go on if she didn't, so she has to make it.

She is lying beside me on the couch in the living room with her head on my chest. I think she's having a hard time falling asleep which doesn't surprise me. I can't understand why we don't have any leads on her parents' whereabouts yet. With this many immortals and warlocks working together, they should have found something out by now. When we get to Graystone tomorrow, I have a few people I can trust to give me the truth. I've made phone calls to several immortals but nobody is calling me back.

I close my eyes and sync my breathing with hers. A short time later, she falls asleep, and soon after, I follow. Too bad I can't dreamwalk while I'm sleeping. Otherwise, I could try to dig into any information on Sierra's parents.

The sounds and smells of the coffee maker wakes us up. All things considered, I actually slept good last night and feel well rested. I think I owe that to being so close to Sierra and knowing she was safe. We have a long day ahead of us, though.

"Good morning beautiful, how did you sleep?" I ask her as she stirs.

"Good morning handsome. I slept well, and you?"

"I slept good. I sleep better when I'm with you." We both sit up and stretch.

"Me too. Let's do that more often." She winks at me.

"I would have to agree with you, Ms. Walker," I say as we head for the delicious scent of fresh coffee and something else. I can't quite put my finger on it.

"Mmmm, that smells amazing. What are you making?" she asks her aunt.

"French toast silly. You always beg me to make it every time you come."

"Of course. Dante, you've never had French toast until you've had my aunt's." Sierra grins at me.

"I can't wait." I smile back at her. I pull out a chair at the table for Sierra to sit while I make us each a cup of coffee. I offer to help Grace but she shooed me away. Feeling dismissed, I sit at the table with Sierra and sip my coffee. I don't see Joe, so I assume he's still asleep.

Then I realize I'm wrong because he shouts from the other room, "Hey! Make sure you save some for me!" Making all three of us laugh.

"Well, you better hurry then!" Grace calls back to him.

"How are you feeling, Sierra?" Joe walks into the kitchen.

"Good, ready to get this over with though."

"Grace and I will be coming with you guys when you leave. So, if you need anything at all we will be there," Joe says to Sierra.

"You don't have to do that. I know how much of a risk it will be for you," Sierra argues.

"We'll be fine. I will not miss my only niece going through the transition. And besides, I think Dante will appreciate the company," Joe says, and I know what he means by that. She may be the one going through the transition, but I'll be the one watching her in pain and waiting to see if her transformation goes- okay. Some immortals have woken up eight hours later and then some others can take up to forty-eight hours. That will be hell for me to just sit by and wait.

"I would appreciate the company, thank you." My eyes meet his.

"Thank you both for everything these last few days. And thank you for coming to make sure he stays out of trouble." Sierra points toward me.

"I'm not the one who goes and finds trouble, my dear," I say playfully to her.

Grace starts bringing plates to the table and we all instantly dig in. If I thought the smell was amazing, I don't have a strong enough word for the taste.

"These taste delicious Grace and are truly amazing. Thank you."

"You are most welcome, Dante."

We finish eating, and I help Joe clean up the dirty dishes. Suddenly, I am starting to think that maybe it's not a good idea for her to go through the transition yet. What if Sierra only chose this because her parents have been taken? What if she regrets it after? I guess how I felt wasn't hard to see because she comes up to me.

"Hey, everything's going to be okay. You'll see, we got this." Sierra gives me a hug.

I hug her back and murmur in her ear, "I love you."

"I love you too," she whispers back to me.

"Are we all ready?" Joe puts the last of the dishes away.

"Yes," we all say.

"We will go first so there are no surprises. Town square?" I ask Joe.

"Yes, we'll follow behind you." Joe grabs his luggage.

I take out my wand-shaped blue benitoite portal stone and point it in the center of the light green living room. I picture in my mind the town square in Graystone and the large circular water fountain in the center. As I create a portal to Graystone, Sierra's eyes go wide with excitement. Once I can see the fountain through the portal I create, I grab her hand, and we both step through and land in the heart of Graystone.

If I thought she was excited before, that was nothing. Joy lights up her face as she takes in the scene around us. Children are running around chasing magical purple butterflies that a young witch in a blue dress has manifested. Eyes wide with wonder, Sierra looks at me then back at the witch. I guess that is one good thing to come out of this; I get to witness her seeing magic for the first time. On the other side of the courtyard, a couple makes a wish and throws a penny into the fountain. Mouth open wide, she glances around at all of the shops with their doors open wide.

"This place is amazing!" she says to me.

"I'm glad you like it," I say, feeling very proud. I've always loved calling this place my home.

Joe and Grace step through next and I take a moment to close the doorway to Ireland and tuck my portal stone safely in my pocket. Grace starts looking all around the courtyard the same way Sierra just did. Unfortunately for her, though, we don't have much time to explore. Immortal enforcers surround us as I knew they would. That's a good and bad thing about Graystone, the immortal enforcers know anybody who arrives or leaves immediately. There's no sneaking anybody in or out without the enforcer's knowledge. But I guess that's not a bad thing. It just reinforces the stories Michael and Joe have told me, how did the High Council not know about Excalibur? The immortal enforcers are the ones who actually implement the laws and protect Graystone. The High Council just does the judging part.

"Joseph Walker and your guest, come with us please. Dante you and your guest as well," Asher the lead enforcer commands.

"Yes, sir," we both say at the same time.

That's one thing you learn early on in Graystone: always do what an enforcer wants. We follow Asher, Joe and Grace up front, Sierra and I behind. The remaining enforcers walk behind and beside us. They do not like surprise visits like we've just done. Not only am I bringing an exiled immortal, but I'm bringing a human. This probably wasn't the best move on my part, but I hope they'll understand and show leniency.

"Stay here, I will see if the High Council will see you now." Asher stops in front of a large gray concrete building. We've arrived at the High Court, where they do all of the council business such as meetings, trials and punishments. He disappears through the large steel doors.

"Is everything okay?" Sierra asks me.

"They just don't know you two, and Joe being exiled, well that complicates things. We just have to talk to the High Council, but it's fine," I say, hoping I'm right. Just then the big black steel doors open.

"The High Council will see you now, follow me." Asher leads us into the building and down a corridor. He opens another steel door and gestures for us to go through as he stands just inside the doorway. I have never been inside this room before, the tall white walls and floor-to-ceiling windows make the room feel enormous. All seven council members were sitting side by side with Ryker in the center. The council members are all very old powerful immortals, nobody really knows their ages or what gifts they may have.

"Joseph Walker, I am surprised to see you here," Ryker's booming voice echoes off the tall ceilings.

"Hello Ryker, councilmen and councilwomen. I am sorry for the intrusion. As you are all aware of the havoc Excalibur has been causing with humans, he has also taken my brother, Michael, and his wife, Sophia. My story is for another day, though." Joe gestures to his right. This is my niece, Sierra Walker, daughter of Michael and Sophia. Sierra is of age and wishes to go through the transition. As I am the only blood relative, other than her kidnapped parents, she has of her knowledge, I am requesting your permission to witness her transition."

"And why should we let you be witness when you abandoned your guardian's oath?" Ryker asks him with calculating eyes.

Sierra's squeezing my hand so hard I think I may lose circulation in it. I want to reassure her, but right now isn't the time.

"I did not abandon my oath. I had to put it on pause while Excalibur's unlawful actions were hidden from others. But I have another witness to Excalibur's deeds with Dante. I always planned to come back, but I could not sit by and watch as more fellow immortal guardians, family or humans were picked off and murdered because of a choice that Michael, Sophia and I made. I knew it was a matter of time before Excalibur showed to you what a monster he truly is, and only now do I hope that you can understand why we left." I must agree that was a compelling argument.

"And you thought bringing a human here will help your case?" Ryker eyes Grace.

"She is my anima gemelli. I could not leave her behind when Excalibur could take her as well. Seeing as he is taking those who turned him in, I assumed I would be next," Joe says.

"But you broke our first rule of being an immortal by telling her what you were." Ryker lifts a disdainful brow, clearly uncaring if Grace is taken. He glances at the other council members in the room who sit silently like statues.

"Not exactly, according to the Immortal Code extenuating circumstances allow it if the human is in imminent danger or is an anima gemella to an immortal," Joe states. An anima gemella is not something the council would be able to get proof of so they have to take him at his word.

"Very well then, Sierra, how long have you known about immortals?" Ryker turns his attention to her.

"Less than a week, sir," Sierra says politely.

"And why do you want to go through the transition?"

"Ever since I was young, I felt that I was meant for more, to do something important. I never felt that I was where I belonged. And then my parents were taken, and I was told what I am or what I could be, that is. Then everything seemed to make sense. I want to help find my parents, but more importantly I want to be somebody that matters. I want to do something for the greater good," Sierra says. If only she could know how much she matters to me.

"Spoken like a true immortal guardian. Give us the room while we discuss the outcome of this visit." Ryker dismisses us. Asher opens the door as we exit and shows us to the benches in the hall. He then goes back into the council room.

Now I know why those doors are steel; you can't hear anything that's going on in there. I don't think I have ever been more nervous than I am right now. Sierra is picking at her nails, so I know she is too. I glance over to Joe, and he nods at me. Joe had valid points for escaping into the human world and Sierra sounded just as good, so I just hope the High Council gives them a chance. We sit out in the corridor for about ten minutes before Asher comes back out.

"The High Council will see you now." He sounds like a recording.

Single file, we all walk into the large council room and stand side by side awaiting whatever judgement they will give.

"The High Council has reviewed your case and has decided to allow Joseph and Grace Walker to bear witness to the transition of Sierra Walker. That is if Sierra passes all of the mandatory pretransition qualifications. Sierra if you pass those and transition into an immortal, you will be required to pledge yourself as an immortal guardian. Are you prepared for that?" Ryker asks.

"Yes, I am, sir," Sierra answers.

"And you realize that will start immediately?"

"Yes."

"You will have four hours to prepare before your pretransition qualifications. The evaluation will be held at the Guardian Academy. Dante, I trust that you can show her the way?" Ryker turns his steely gaze to me.

"Of course," I answer him.

"Carry on then," Ryker says.

SIERRA

Well, that was scary having to say all that in front of them. I've always hated having to do a presentation at school, but this was on a whole other level. It was kind of creepy that they were all dressed in black robes like the Grim Reaper. I couldn't wait to get out of there, having seven really old immortals judging me was very uncomfortable, especially knowing how they felt about my parents. The High Council members were the ones that put my parents in this situation in the first place. They should have dealt with Excalibur a long time ago.

We walk out of the large steel doors into the warm sunshine, and I am immediately taken aback by the number of immortals and or witches and warlocks there are around us. I can't believe I have been so blind for so long. As soon as we are off the steps to the building, we move off to the side to get out of the way of anybody walking by.

"Do you remember everything we told you about the qualifications?" Uncle Joe asks.

"I believe so." I nod.

"Okay, I think we should take a little bit of time and go over the Immortal Code," Uncle Joe says.

"I think I have those down pact."

"Really what's number four?"

"Always fill out the required paperwork immediately after the incident," I say, proving I know it to him.

"Nice job, number two?" Uncle Joe fires back.

"Only use your gifts for good. I told you I knew them. I've been studying the book."

"Good job. Dante, how about we head to the field to do some practice maneuvers?" Uncle Joe asks him.

"That sounds like a good idea to me." Dante reaches for my hand. He leads me down one road and then another, and finally we get to a large stone building. After we walk down the cobblestone driveway toward the back of the building, I find us on the edge of a large field. Several people are spread out, broken up into pairs and are sparring with each other.

"This building is the Guardian Academy and these are all students training. I know your parents taught you quite a bit but we'll go over the basics that you will need to know," Dante says.

"Game on," I taunt.

"I'll take it easy on you." He's goading me.

"Good." I don't think he knows just how much training my parents have done with me.

"Follow my lead and do as I do, okay?"

"Will do."

We go through a few basic moves and stances, and he seems surprised by which ones I get right off.

"Very good, do you think you're ready to spar with me?" He has a twinkle in his eye.

"Am I ever." I wink back.

"Make sure you're ready because I am not going to be easy. You see them over there? That's what they will expect in your pretransition qualification." He points out toward the other students. They are not just sparring, those immortals are landing kicks, punches and other blows directly to their partner. I watch as one of the kids are kicked hard enough in the chest to send him backward with a hard landing flat on his back. A second later he jumps back up for more.

"I'm ready," I say, hoping it's true. I'm still a little sore where my aunt had to put stitches in my back. Aunt Grace and Uncle Joe take a seat in the grass to watch us.

We go at it a few times, and I can tell he's holding back. He's not hitting me like the students across the field are landing blows with their opponent. I'm able to swing my leg against the back of his knees, his legs buckle and his eyes grow wide, but he manages to bounce back up with the help of a hand to the ground. He was not expecting that. The sight makes me giggle. Next thing I know, I'm on the ground flat on my back. I don't even know how I got there, but I can hear Uncle Joe in the background laughing. No doubt because I got cocky by surprising Dante and let my guard down. Yup, my back is tender for sure. I grit my teeth through the searing pain that landing causes.

"You okay?" Dante asks, concern written all over his face as he holds out his hand to help me up.

"Yes, that wasn't fair though." I'm laughing as I grab his hand.

"Well, I hate to break it to you babe, but the bad guys don't play fair so you need to be ready." Dante gets ready to go again by planting his feet firmly on the ground.

We spar with each other for close to an hour back and forth. I do manage to land a few strikes on him. Not anywhere close to the amount he did on me though. But he seemed happy with my skills, all things considered.

"Are you hungry?"

"Yes. How about you?" I brush the dirt off of my clothing.

"Very. They have a pizza place about two blocks away. How's that sound?" Dante wipes his hands on the pantleg of his blue jeans.

"You had me at pizza," I say.

"Pizza always sounds good." Aunt Grace has joined us with Uncle Joe.

"I agree." Uncle Joe wraps an arm around his wife.

We all head down the cobblestone driveway but when we get to the road, we took a right instead. We travel down the street, a number of people stare at us. No doubt wondering who I am, and they probably know Uncle Joe. I catch some of the women staring at Dante. The others don't seem fazed by the onlookers, but it's really starting to bother me. I hate nosy people.

Ten minutes later, when Dante gets the door to the restaurant, a waitress with multiple facial piercings and pale skin greets us.

"Hi Dante, how many in your party?" she asks, her gaze lingering longer than I'd like on him.

"Hi Sharon. It's four today." He grabs my hand again.

"Follow me." She sniffs and looks away, clearly taking the hint. She leads us to a little black booth in the back of the restaurant and puts four menus on the table. "I'll give you guys a few minutes to look it over."

I grab the little brown menu that says Chief's Pizza House and flip it over. They have so many options here; every type of pizza or calzone you can imagine is listed. My mouth is watering at the thought of all that doughy cheesy miracle food.

"Just remember you have more training, so you can't pig out." Uncle Joe starts to laugh. It must have been obvious I was a little disappointed I couldn't eat everything I wanted.

"We can always come back later. I thought you would like it here." Dante gives me an amused smile.

It didn't even dawn on me before but this is the first time we have actually gone out of the house together. Is this our first date? Hmm. Kind of strange with my aunt and uncle.

"I think I'd like that." I give him a smile back. He puts his arm around my shoulder and pulls me closer. Heat radiates off him in waves, even in the dream realm. I'm going to start thinking of him as my personal heater. The waiter comes back and notices his arm around me and she narrows her eyes at me and there's a definite curl to her lip. She went from a little put off to snobby in an instant. Dante doesn't seem to care, though I want to ask him what the deal is with her later. Uncle Joe and Aunt Grace return from the restroom in time to place our order with the stuck-up waitress.

"We have about two hours before your qualification so I think we should do a little more training to make sure you pass," Uncle Joe says.

"This time with you, old man?" I straighten up in my seat.

"Hey now, I may be older but that doesn't mean I can't give you a beat down." He challenges me back.

"Fair enough, but I bet you're out of practice." I bait him.

"While that may be true, I have some tricks that the academy doesn't teach you," he says.

We eat our meal with little interruption from the waitress and are on our way with only about an hour and a half left. I'm starting to get anxious. What if I am not good enough to pass? Will my next round of training with my uncle help me pass?

Dante must have been able to tell my nerves were shot because he squeezes my hand as we were walking along the sidewalk. "You're going to do fine. Try not to worry too much."

"Can you read minds too?" I ask, only half-joking.

"No, but I can tell when something's bothering you. When you doubt yourself, that's when you will make a mistake. You'll be amazing as usual, just remember that." Dante then whispers in my ear, "I can always give you private lessons with just us." Then he winks at me, and I can't help the feeling of my cheeks warming. He smiles as if knowing how much just the thought affects me. I feel guilty that I'm enjoying my time with Dante knowing my parents are out there somewhere.

"Are you saying I should be horrible so I can have extra lessons?" I whisper back.

"Well, you should be good for your qualification. There's always something extra you can learn after, though." He plays along.

We get back to the field, my uncle bounces back and forth from one foot to the other. "Let's do this, Sierra."

"Are you ready?" Not waiting for him to answer, I take a jab at him with my fist on his lower abdomen and land it.

"That was cheap." He takes a swing at my side and misses.

I try not to get arrogant again. It's clear he's been out of it for some time. He's not as quick or fierce as Dante. Which is kind of nice to be on the upside. The next thing I know, he lands a kick to my stomach and I fall backward not able to catch myself.

"Get back up, let's go," Uncle Joe demands.

I jump to my feet and swipe my foot against his ankle and knock him down. We go back and forth for about twenty minutes. Then we take about a five-minute break. My uncle rests his hands on his thighs and bends over, out of breath. Dante comes up to me with one of those pink elixirs I've seen him drinking the last few days. He hands it over to me, already open.

"Take a drink of this. It'll help you be a little stronger, and your muscles won't ache as much."

"I thought only full immortals could drink these?" I ask him.

"They benefit us a lot more than a pretransition immortal, but it will still help you quite a bit. It's loaded with vitamins and minerals your body needs to train this hard," he explains to me.

"Not bad." This time I don't smell it first; I just drink it. I find it's actually pretty good and tastes a lot like a strawberry banana smoothie.

"Now it's my turn. Are you ready to go again?"

"Sure." I screw the cap back on my drink, set it down, and head to the spot we've been practicing. He lets me warm up a bit before he starts getting rougher. I focus on using my smaller size as a benefit and slip out of his way, but he catches on to that trick quickly. I start getting tired, even with the elixir. I'm not used to doing this for this long at a time. Not to mention I'm still healing from the plane incident.

He takes me down three times in a row, but the last time I yank him down with me. He lands on top of me, managing not to crush me, but his lips are just inches from mine, and we pause there like that. Until a throat clears.

"Okay, let's go, love birds. It doesn't take that long to get up. I think we can call it a day," Uncle Joe says, clearly not finding us amusing.

We both start laughing. Dante gets up first and helps me up, and pulls me right into his arms. He kisses me in front of my aunt and uncle, and I kiss him back, not caring about the grumbles I can hear in the background.

"We should probably go get her registered for her evaluation," Uncle Joe says.

"Oh, give them a minute. They're not hurting anything," Aunt Grace chides him.

Dante breaks off the kiss and says only loud enough for me to hear, "I'm sorry if I was too rough on you."

"You weren't. It's okay. I could tell you were still holding back."

"I didn't want to hurt you. I know your parents taught you well, but years of combat with actual enemies is a different type of fighting," Dante says.

"Thank you for helping and supporting me."

"Anything for you." He looks down at me with warm eyes.

We walk to the front of the Guardian Academy, through the large wooden door, and inside. We head over to an old worn desk to the right, where a man sits, wearing the same blue uniform as the immortal enforcers from earlier. I'm instantly on edge now.

"Can I help you?" he asks in a deep voice looking up from his paperwork.

"My name is Sierra Walker. I have a pretransition qualification evaluation scheduled at three." I try to sound like I belong here. That is a mouthful to say when you're nervous. His brown eyes on me feel like they can see into my soul. It's very uncomfortable and I'm grateful when he looks back down at his desk.

"I see you on the list. Follow me. Your guests must stay here, though. I'll give you a moment to part ways." He turns around to give us privacy.

Uncle Joe and Aunt Grace step up first, giving me a big, tight hug and squeeze.

"Good luck sweetheart, I know your parents would be proud," Aunt Grace says.

"You have this Sierra. We believe in you. You can do this. We'll see you in a little while." Uncle Joe sounds proud.

"Thank you both so much. I love you guys." I swipe at my eyes trying not to cry.

"And we love you." They both step outside to give Dante and I some time together.

"Come here you." Dante tugs me into his arms and kisses me with no regard to the nearby enforcer.

"Thank you for helping me," I say again.

"You're welcome baby. Remember to stay out of your head. You're smart and quick on your feet. You can do this. I have faith in you. I love you, and I will be right outside when you pass." He gives me a quick pep talk.

"I love you too, handsome." I hug him one last time before he turns away.

Just before he gets to the door, he turns around and gives me a smile that makes my knees go weak. How is he able to affect me this much? And he knows he can, so I think he takes advantage of that. I smile back what I hope is equally charming to him. I turn and walk toward the enforcer. I hope I'm ready for this evaluation.

CHAPTER 13

SIERRA

As I follow the enforcer down the long empty corridor it feels like my stomach is in my throat. Our footsteps echoing off the walls is making me more antsy. He stops next to a set of large wooden double doors and opens one of them as he steps through.

"Audrey, I have Ms. Walker here," he calls into the large open room.

"Hello, Ms. Walker. I will be doing your evaluation today." The woman who appears from inside the training room has an athletic build with long braided black hair. She nods at the man who brought me here and he leaves, closing the door behind him. Audrey shows me where I can set my stuff and goes over the expectations with me.

I follow her to the section of the room with the gray padded floor mats are. I stand with my feet shoulder width apart and take a deep breath. My arms instinctively fly in front of my face, blocking the punch Audrey just tried to land. I expected her to warn me first. She swings her other fist and lands a hard blow to my lower abdomen. I try to swing a hook at her chin but she catches my fist in her hand, I kick my leg to her opposite side and my foot lands on Audrey's hip. She's quick and has better reflexes than I do.

She takes a step back and bounces on the balls of her feet like a boxer. She kicks at me and I back away just in time so she misses. We alternate turns of striking, dodging and sometimes succeeding but after about 20 minutes my muscles are tired and I'm starting to slow down. She takes advantage of that weakness. Her fist collides with my face and the blow causes me to lose my balance. She slams her foot hard into my ribs and the force knocks me on my back. The wind is sucked from my lungs. The metallic taste of blood fills my mouth, and the strong scent of Lysol from the mats makes my eyes sting.

"Get up!" Audrey yells.

I jump to my feet in time to duck another of her powerful blows. Get out of your head, you can do this. Your parents are counting on you. All the rage I've been carrying about my mom and dad being kidnapped, the lies my parents told me, having my memories stolen and the lack of results from the investigation finally reached a boiling point. I let out a frustrated scream as I barrel toward Audrey and my fists and feet finally make contact. I don't know how many times I hit her or where the collisions took place.

"Okay, okay, stop!" All of a sudden, I'm struggling to breathe, standing over Audrey on the mat and she's scrambling to get up. Her eyes wide as she takes a step back from me. "You alright?"

"Yes, I-I'm sorry. I didn't mean to do that." I cover my mouth, shocked at what just happened. "I didn't hurt you, did I?"

"You did, but that's okay. All the anger that you have, bottle that and save it for when you need to use it like you just did. That fury will help you in the field with the dark ones."

I didn't realize I'm holding on to that much anger within me, I've never lashed out like that before. I feel bad for hurting her, but to be fair she hurt me too. I think she's done doing hand-to-hand combat with me for now because she walks over to the wall with the fencing gear hanging on it. We each put all the needed equipment over our clothing to keep us safe.

We duel in silence for a while and I'm reminded of the past when my mom and I would fence together. My body may be tired but I have muscle memory which helps me to hold my own with Audrey. The vinegar-like scent of sweat in my mask makes me wonder how often they clean these or if it's me that smells that bad. I'm trying to think of anything I can other than what's at stake if I fail.

Audrey stops me from advancing on her and moves me on to the next task, the treadmill. There is a preset workout loaded into the machine that I need to be able to accomplish to prove that I have the stamina to be able to fight like an immortal guardian. I try to drink water to stay hydrated but it feels like the water will come back up. The path is uphill, downhill, fast, then slow. Just when I start getting used to the pace or the incline, the program changes. My legs are heavy and unsteady, it's getting hard to keep up. What if I'm not cut out to be a guardian, or even a full immortal? How much more can I take before my body gives up?

The treadmill finally switches to the cool-down mode signaling that this torture is almost over. Now that my body has been thoroughly exhausted Audrey offers for me to take a seat as she drills me about the Immortal Code and the various dark ones. She disappears into a small room next to the mats. Audrey reappears with a Gatorade and a protein bar in her hand that she gives me. I sit quietly while she is looking through the papers she's been using while asking me questions. I can't fail, not when I've come this far.

DANTE

After I leave Sierra and step out into the blazing sun, the reality of what is happening finally hits me. My Sierra is trying to become one of us. I had hoped this day would come, but I had wanted to be able to prepare her more for the prequalification. My anxiety must be written all over my face because as soon as Grace sees me come out, she wraps a pair of comforting arms around me.

"She will do great. She's very stubborn, and she's had several great role models and trainers to help guide her. Try not to worry too much, dear," Grace says in a soothing tone.

"I know. I just wish I had more time to help her. All of this seems so sudden." I crack my knuckles out of habit.

"There never is enough time, but you did the best you could do. She really loves you, you know?"

"I know, and I love her more than anything." I reach up and grasp my amulet that matches hers.

"So why don't we go into town and pick her up something nice while we wait?" Grace suggests.

"That's a great idea, Grace. She will need a dress for the transition ceremony too." The lines by Joe's eyes crinkle with a smile.

I know they were just trying to get me to stop worrying, but I'm not sure it's going to work. A normal prequalification evaluation takes about three hours to complete. We head into town and pick out a few things we think Sierra will like. I agree to meet up with her aunt and uncle at the bookstore down the road, there's somebody I need to stop in and see. I head in the opposite direction than Joe and Grace and arrive at Gerard's pub.

I talk to the bartender who vanishes behind the bar to see if Gerard will see me. Gerard usually knows everything that's going on in Graystone and I happen to be one of the few he likes. He's a grumpy older immortal who doesn't take any crap from anybody and isn't afraid of ruffling somebody's feathers.

"It's been a while Dante, what rock have you been hiding under?" The short stout man hobbles his way out from the back room.

"I know it's been quite some time, I've been pretty busy lately."

"Well, come on back boy."

I follow Gerard to his office and start to tell him what I can about Excalibur and the situation I've found myself in. As soon as he hears Excalibur's name, he quickly holds a finger up for me to wait and he turns some music on.

"There's ears everywhere," he whispers as he slides his chair closer to mine. "Something is off about that Master Council Ryker."

I know I can trust him so I divulge on some information that Joe and Michael have told me. Gerard didn't seem surprised at all by the story and informed me that after Michael, Sophia and Joe left Graystone, other immortal guardians have been asked to enlist with Excalibur's group, the Revolution. Not all of them joined, and the ones who didn't join him, disappeared as well. The others either vanished on their own like Sierra's family or foul play was suspected.

Some of the noble guardians who declined Excalibur's offer also reported the evil man to the High Council for treason. Gerard believes that the High Council is covering it up since there is no paper trail of the other immortal guardians reporting him and clearly they haven't taken care of the issue. Gerard's business partner Frank was very public about why he thought no justice was served for the missing or the dead, the next day he died in a car accident. Awfully convenient timing.

It doesn't seem like the High Council will actually investigate Excalibur. I'm starting to think they're just blowing smoke up my ass. Gerard's going to put some feelers out to his contacts to find out more information. We part ways and agree to meet up again soon.

On my way to meet Joe and Grace a window display catches my eye. The bracelet consists of a dainty silver chain with five small seashell charms. Thinking Sierra will love it, I decide to get it for her.

Once purchased, I step back out into the heat and check my watch. We still have about an hour left until Sierra is done with her evaluation. I head into the bookshop next door. It doesn't take me long to spot them with Grace's flaming red hair.

"Hello Dante, how have you been?" a familiar voice asks.

I turn around and find my ex-girlfriend behind me. We dated on and off for a few years. Nothing was wrong with her; she just wasn't the one. I think she took the breakup harder than I did. Last I knew, she was transferred to Canada. "Oh, hi Marissa, I'm doing good. And you?"

"I'm doing okay. Is there anything I can help you find?" she asks me, with unmistakable longing in her eyes as she pulls several strands of brown hair around one ear.

"No, thanks. I'm just here to meet some people." I hope she'll give me some space. I feel bad for hurting her, but she knew going into it that I had an anima gemelli. I've always loved Sierra, but she was young and I was a man. Even though Sierra wasn't old enough to date, it always kind of felt like I was cheating on her by being with other women, which never sat right with me.

"Okay, let me know if you change your mind," she says before moving back toward the counter.

I walk over to Joe and Grace.

"I found a few books that I think Sierra would find helpful." Joe nods to several hardbacks in his hands.

"Sounds like a good idea. We should probably start heading back to the academy in case she gets out earlier." I run a hand through my hair. My conversation with Gerard keeps replaying in my mind. I'll wait until later on tonight to fill the others in.

"I agree, I don't want her to come out and not have anybody there," Grace says.

Luckily when we get to the academy, she isn't out yet. So, we sit on the front steps and just wait. It feels like forever before she finally comes through the doors looking pretty beat.

SIERRA

"**H**ey beautiful." Dante gets up from the front steps.

"Hey handsome," I reply as he embraces me.

"So, how did it go?" Uncle Joe asks me, obviously wanting to get right to the point.

I still can't believe it as I tell them, "It was rough, but I passed." They all look relieved.

"I didn't doubt you for a moment. Did they schedule the transition?" Uncle Joe's smile broadens.

"Yes, it's on Thursday. They said I got in just in time for this month's full moon. It's the last pod they have available." That means I only have one free day before I make the transition.

"Congratulations!" Aunt Grace gives me a quick hug.

"I'm so proud of you. I knew you could do it. Would you like to grab some take-out and head back to my place and rest?"

"That sounds good to me." I am so sore and tired, but my stomach's growling isn't going to let me sleep until I get something in it.

We decide on calzones and my mouth is watering just thinking about them. We all start walking in that direction, and I think Dante can tell I'm tired because he offers to have me piggyback on him. I decline; I need to prove to everybody that I can do this. I'm glad once we get to the pizza place that Sharon is nowhere in sight. I don't think I have the energy to pretend to be nice to her again.

We place our order with the nice blonde working up front and wait outside until they call Dante's name. After we grab our dinner and walk a little way from the building, Dante creates another portal. This time I recognize what's on the other side—his home. I step through the portal and onto his front porch. I don't think I will ever get used to traveling like immortals.

After everyone is on the other side, Dante closes the portal and digs his key out of his pocket to open the door. Looking around his place as I walk through and toward the kitchen, I notice some long swords hung on the wall next to a few trophies that weren't there in the dream realm. I move closer to the trophies and read them. First place for swordsmanship, another said second place for marksmanship. I can't say that I'm surprised; just from what I saw training with him, he would be a very fierce opponent. I kind of feel bad for whoever has to go up against him.

Dante walks into the kitchen and sets the take-out bags on his stone-colored countertop. He takes out some plates from a cupboard just above them and hands them out along with each person's calzone box. We chat a little as we eat but just simple conversation, nothing heavy.

"What are we going to do tomorrow?" I ask.

"Whatever you want to do. We could go into town and show you around. They also have a sand beach close to the town we can check out," Dante offers.

"That sounds like a plan to me," I say, yawning. From what I have seen, this place is pretty amazing. I wish my parents were here with me as well, though.

"Why don't we all call it a night and get some sleep?" Uncle Joe asks after finishing the last of his food.

"I can't wait to sleep." I yawn again.

"Oh, I almost forgot we found something in town that may help you." Aunt Grace reaches behind her for a little brown shopping bag and she hands it over to me. "We stopped by this adorable little bookshop in town and found you some books that may help you to learn more before your final qualification evaluation."

"Awe, thank you. You guys didn't have to get me anything." I hug her.

"It's okay. We wanted to." Uncle Joe hugs me as well.

I open the bag and look through the books. I find the first two to be about demons and dark ones, the next on fighting techniques, and last but not least one gets into crystals and potions, which excites me the most.

"I have something for you as well." Dante offers me a large white box with a purple ribbon bow around it. "Your aunt and uncle helped me pick it out."

Aunt Grace chuckles. "Oh, don't even. That was all you. We just agreed."

I gingerly open it, not knowing what to expect. Once I get the cover off and look inside, I lift a dress by the shoulder straps from the box. It is a long white bohemian style flowy dress, and it's gorgeous. It is one of those things you don't know you need until you see it.

"Wow, Dante, this is beautiful. Thank you! Now you're going to have to bring me someplace fancy so I can wear it." I send him a cheeky wink.

"Your very welcome. I'm glad you like it. We also got you these to match." He gives me another smaller shoe box.

I lift the lid and find inside a pair of cute white strappy dress shoes with small heels. They match perfectly with the dress.

"You didn't need to do that handsome," I say as I give him a quick peck on the cheek.

"Well, I wanted to. And besides, you will need it for the transition ceremony. But I do plan on taking you out someplace fancy soon." He winks back.

"Well, it sounds like we're going to have a long day tomorrow. Dante, do you mind showing us to our room?" Uncle Joe asks. I think him seeing the gushy stuff we do makes him uncomfortable. I kind of want to do it more just to get to him. He's aggravated me plenty of times; now it's my turn.

"Sure thing," Dante answers as we say our goodnights to each other.

Dante leads them from the room and they disappear down the hallway. Finally, I have a moment to just breathe. Time is moving so fast. Dante reappears a minute later, and I didn't realize just how tired he looks until now. He has dark circles under his eyes.

"Hey handsome, are you okay?" I ask him.

"I am now that you're here."

"You look tired."

"I am. It's been a long day. I knew you could pass. I just wish we had more time, so it didn't take this much out of you." His eyes darken with worry.

"It's okay, and I'm okay I promise," I say to him. "I'm glad you were here with me."

"There's no place I would rather be." He takes my hand. "Let's get you to bed."

He leads me by the hand to his bedroom, which just the thought of going to his bedroom is giving me butterflies. We have only been in the living room and the kitchen in the dream realm, so this will be all new. Once we step inside, I can't help but notice the large rustic-looking log bed in the middle of the room. Right next to it is a matching nightstand with a large eight by ten picture framed photograph of me laughing. I don't recognize that photo, but I look really happy in it.

He shuts the door behind us, and he notices that I see it. "You are the joy in my life. No matter how bad my day is, if I come home and see that picture of you, it makes the day more bearable."

"You don't have to explain. If I had a picture of you, I would have it next to my bed as well," I say honestly.

"Would you like one of my shirts to sleep in? I'm sorry I didn't think to pick up any other clothes for you," Dante says.

"Sure, it's okay, really. I can pick up some stuff tomorrow."

"Or you could sleep without..." He trails off as he comes over to me and starts kissing me.

"That might not be a good idea since my aunt and uncle are down the hall." I kiss him back, wishing I wasn't so tired.

"I'll go grab that shirt for you." He breaks away from me. Dante goes into his closet and grabs a black t-shirt with *Metallica* written in silver on it and a pair of black boxers. I swear all he wears is black shirts. Which is fine by me because he looks amazing in them.

"Thank you, do you mind if I take a quick shower?" I ask as I grab the clothes and step toward the bathroom attached to the master bedroom. I got pretty sweaty and gross today at the evaluation.

"You're welcome, and take all the time you need."

I start the water and hop in. I shower as quickly as I can and got dressed. The boxers are big on me, which is no surprise, so I just roll the hem a few times to make them fit better. The shirt is made out of the softest cotton I have ever felt. It's also a little big, but it is very comfortable. I'm glad Aunt Grace had packed a few things for me, such as a toothbrush and a hair brush.

I step out of the bathroom to the sight of Dante wearing nothing but boxers and lying on the top of the covers of his bed. Man, I can get used to seeing that every day. He's eyeing me from head to toe with eyes full of wanting. I meet his gaze as I walk closer to the bed.

"This shirt is so soft," I murmur, trying to think of what to say.

"It's my favorite, but it looks much better on you," his voice grows husky.

"Somehow I doubt that." I sit on the bed next to him. He pulls the blankets up so we can both get under the covers, and then reaches next to the bed to shut the lamp off. I roll onto my side so I can snuggle against him and he wraps his arms around me.

"Goodnight, beautiful." He kisses the top of my head.

"Goodnight handsome," I reply, and that's the last thing I remember before sleep claims me.

CHAPTER 14

MICHAEL

Excalibur is keeping us in a small cell in the basement of what I gather is a castle or a large stone building of some sort. Sophia and I are both bound by iron chains in separate cells right next to each other. I have been counting the days by making tally marks in the dirt under the bed. Very little light is able to come into my cell, which means I have a limited timeframe to add tallies. I see the sun in the morning for a short while, so that means I'm in an east-facing cell.

If my counting is right, we have been here for seven days. I can't imagine what Sierra has gone through this last week. She had to have survived the plane crash since Dante was there. I feel bad that we are not there to help guide her, but I would make the same choice if I had to do it again. I don't want Excalibur getting his hands on her. It's bad enough he has Sophia and me, but at least we've had a good run. We have the training and the know-how of dealing with situations like this.

Excalibur has come down to the cell block a few times since we've been here to check on things. There are a few others prisoners from what I can tell, but I can't be sure. He keeps us in iron, so we can't use any of our abilities, not like they would help us while we're chained anyways. Sophia's gift is swordsmanship, and neither one of us have been able to get near a dagger, sword, or similar weapon. My visions or premonitions could possibly help if there were a way to get out. After how many visions I had leading up to this, though, it's nice to get a break from them. The migraines that follow are excruciating. I hope the High Council will now be forced to take him down since he hijacked a plane of humans. But I believe the High Council has been glamoured before by Excalibur, so why would this time be any different? I hate to be cynical, but I don't think they'll be coming to rescue us.

There has been one hell of a revelation since we've been captured. Raymond and his wife Charlotte, Emma's parents, are involved with Excalibur. The only way I know this is because Charlotte has been taking vials of our blood for "testing." Whatever that means. I wouldn't put it past Excalibur to poison us or use us as experiments for some sick twisted game. Sophia and I have tried to talk to her, but she's always escorted by another traitor immortal and will not speak unless giving us direct orders about the blood draw.

I can't believe we didn't know. I feel like an idiot; I should've sensed something. I really hope Emma is not involved with Excalibur. That will be what will break Sierra. She loves her like a sister, although I wonder if their relationship was forced on Emma without her even knowing. I had heard that Excalibur was able to mind control some of his followers from another prisoner. That could explain why the High Council didn't have him arrested in the past. I have yet to see Raymond. The coward is sending his wife down here while he hides upstairs. I want to get my hands on that son of a bitch.

Excalibur has demanded to know the whereabouts of Joe and Sierra and what gifts we have along with other immortals associated with us. I've given him nothing even after he's tortured me by cutting, branding and whipping me. Name it, he'll try it. I can take it, but I'm afraid I'll crack if he uses those methods on Sophia. So far, he hasn't been nearly as rough with her as he has been with me. Which I am glad for.

Most of the time, the prisoners are alone down here with just one guard at the entrance. Depending on who the guard is dictates whether we get food. Most of the guards despise us and refuse to give us the necessities. One guard, Theodore, seems like he's trying to help us. He'll give the other prisoners and I extra food and water, knowing that most of the other guards will withhold those items. If there is a weak link in Excalibur's followers, it would be him.

Muffled voices suddenly come from the entrance. One sounds familiar, but I can't place it. They're having some heated argument, but I can't tell the subject. A few moments later, I hear footsteps approaching our dimly lit cells, and the shadow of a man stops in front of mine. I move closer to the bars and realize it's Eric, Emma's older brother.

"What do you want?"

"Listen, I didn't want any part of this. Raymond blackmailed me."

"And I'm just supposed to believe that?" What a typical answer.

"If I didn't do what Raymond and his boss wanted, they said they'd hurt Emma," Eric says in exasperation.

"Was any of it real, all the family barbeques and your friendship with my daughter?" I ask, needing to know the answer.

"I didn't know Raymond and Charlotte were working with Excalibur until I was thirteen, and Emma knows nothing. But I didn't ask for any of this. I've tried to keep Emma and Sierra safe. He promised me he wouldn't hurt Sierra but after he crashed that plane and then I found this," Eric whispers as Sophia and I press against the bars to hear better.

"What did you find?" I wrap my hands around the bars.

"Raymond has been pulling long hours. He sent me to retrieve something from his office and bring it here because he was too busy." Eric takes out his phone and unlocks it. "I came across this. It looks like all the blood they've been taking from all of you was cataloged by your gifts. There are at least one hundred names on this sheet, and they're not all prisoners or associates that work for him."

I look at the list on his phone with our name, gift and blood type. Another column is to the right with only a few marks in it with some type of code I can't make out. Then I see Sierra's name on that list, and my stomach turns to ice.

"Michael, what could the list be for?" Sophia asks me.

"I don't know. I think he might be trying to alter our blood or maybe cancel out our gifts altogether," I say, not knowing what else he could need it for.

"I have to go. I only had five minutes, but I have these for you. They're iron canceling pills. Raymond made me start taking them years ago so that I'd be immune to iron. It takes a few days to build up in your system. I will try to come down again when I can." Eric hands the pills to me.

"Thank you, Eric. Please be careful," Sophia warns him.

"I will, and I really am sorry."

"I know you are. Stay safe," I tell him as he walks away and disappears into the shadows.

After he leaves, I hide the small gray pills under the bed in the darkest corner. They blend right in, and unless you know they are there, you don't see them.

"Do you think he's being truthful or trying to gain our trust?" Sophia whispers to me at the edge of her cell, the stone in between us hindering our ability to communicate easily.

"I think it's both. He doesn't seem like he would be lying. Knowing what I know about his relationship with Raymond, I think he does want to help us. But just to be safe, I'll be the only one taking the pills for the first few days in case it's a trap." I am usually good at reading people, and he seemed spiteful of his dad.

"Are you sure that's a good idea?" Sophia asks me.

"What choice do we have? Our daughter's name was on that sheet as well." I roughly rub my face, not liking that he's able to get his hands on who has what gifts. Sierra hasn't even gone through the transition, nor is it for sure she will.

SIERRA

I wake up to the sound of the birds chirping the following morning. I must have been really tired because it felt like I had just laid down to go to sleep. Dante is still asleep next to me. I don't want to wake him so I try to stay as still as I can and watch him sleep. He looks so peaceful and vulnerable in his sleep, different from the hardened soldier I see while he's awake. It amazes me how sweet and thoughtful he can be toward me. I know yesterday was harder on him than he admits, so I can't imagine how tomorrow will be for him. From everything I've been told and have read, the transition can get pretty bad. I'm glad that Aunt Grace and Uncle Joe will be able to comfort him during that time.

He must have felt me staring at him because he starts moving a little. Then he opens those beautiful eyes of his and searches mine.

"Good morning, beautiful." He sounds groggy.

"Good morning, handsome. How did you sleep?"

"I slept good. How about you?"

"Good." I'm surprised I slept that well with how worried I am about my parents. I feel safe when I sleep next him, but also a little guilty that I am safe when my parents aren't.

"Are you ready to get up?" he asks me.

"Do we have to? I kind of like the idea of staying in bed all day." I smile at him.

"As tempting as that is, I don't think Grace and Joe would appreciate that. There'll be plenty of days we can do that later though," he says, smiling back.

"Well, it was worth a shot." I get up out of bed.

I grab my clothes from yesterday and head toward the bathroom to get ready. By the time I came back out, he's already dressed and sitting on the edge of the bed. I walk over to him and put my arms on his shoulders and slide them around his neck.

"Are you sure you want to go through with the transition?" His brows furrow as he looks up into my eyes.

"Yes, I'm sure." When I see his expression sober, I ask him, "Is everything all right?"

He runs his hands through his hair then places them on my waist. "I just want to make sure you're doing it for you and not because of your parents or me. I don't want you to regret this decision later on."

I have to gather my thoughts before I respond. "I want to be an immortal guardian; I feel like that is what I was born to do. Of course, I want to help with my parents and be able to be with you as well. But those aren't the main reasons I'm doing it," I answer truthfully.

"Okay, because there is no going back." His brows dip as he stares into my eyes.

"I know that." I tip my head down and rest my forehead on his, but he breaks away from me all too soon.

"I thought I'd show you the beach, but we better get going before it gets too crowded."

I follow him out of the bedroom and down the hall into the kitchen. Aunt Grace and Uncle Joe are already there making a pot of coffee. After we eat breakfast, we head into town. We are still waiting to hear back from the High Council and I can't just sit here in this house doing nothing. I need to do something to take my mind off of everything that's out of my control. This time we take Dante's truck so we can see the sights but also leave any shopping bags in the truck as well.

As Dante drives the black Silverado, tall pines surround us on both sides, and I find myself finally taking in the beauty of the island. The trees start thinning the closer we get to town. After an hour of driving, we park in a large parking garage just down the street from the council building.

All the buildings in the area are stone, concrete or brick, and even though maintained throughout the years, the walls are faded from age. Trees line the sidewalk and planters filled with purple, pink, and white flowers bracket several shop windows. Dante said it stays between seventy and ninety degrees all year here, so it's always summertime. We go into a few shops on the main road picking up some things that we all need.

Several people we pass stare at us with unmistakable curiosity. Many seem to know Dante because they stop and talk to him. Most of the people seemed nice enough, though as he introduces us to many of them. The coolest shop we go into is the Alchemist's Palace. The outside of the building is a dark shade of purple, my favorite color. The display case reveals so many types of potions, crystals, and the equipment to use them. I can see myself spending a lot of time and money in here.

After we're all done shopping, we decide to head to Sundial Beach. We all hop back into the truck and head in that direction. Dante had brought his own swim trunks and the rest of us picked up ours at one of the shops in town. As we pull into the parking lot for the beach a bunch of food trucks line the outside edge, giving us a huge selection of options for lunch, but Dante and I settle on an Italian sausage. Uncle Joe and Aunt Grace both get cheeseburgers from a different food truck. We sit at one of the picnic tables overlooking the water while we eat. I can't stop thinking about my parents and what could be happening to them. I'm unable to finish my lunch as thoughts of worse case scenarios run through my mind.

Dante wasn't joking this beach is beautiful. It reminds me of paradise-like travel pictures with a white sand beach and clear turquoise water. I can't wait to go in; I have always loved the ocean. I could lay on a beach all day and just listen to the calming sound of the crashing waves. We dress into our swim suits inside at a building that offers changing rooms alongside bathrooms. I'm so excited to go I almost forgot to spray myself down with sunblock.

Dante and I walk down to the water's edge. The sand is so soft on my feet, and I can see several small seashells along the way. We stop and pick up a few that we like as the warm water laps at our toes. Off in the distance, you can see the large Ferris wheel at the amusement park. I can understand why many immortals live here. I don't think I would want to live anywhere else if had I grown up here. The gorgeous man beside me also has a lot to do with that decision.

Plenty of lounge chairs dot along the beach just out of the reach of the tide. Dante and I claim a pair by setting our towels and clothes on them. It's hard for me to feel okay about having a good time when I don't know if my parents are okay or not. I try not to think about that too much. After I go through the transition, I might actually be able to help. I have spoken to the High Council again about them, and they assured me that they are making headway with the investigation.

One of Dante's friends is on the team of investigators and has been trying to keep Dante updated on what's going on. They still don't have a concrete answer of where they think Excalibur is, but the team believes he's in England. His friend wouldn't elaborate on why he thinks he's there. I just really hope they find them soon. I suspect Excalibur has people on the inside and that they are hindering the investigation. I just have that gut feeling.

I try to let it go and enjoy my last day of being a human. That sounds so strange to me still. I am nervous about what tomorrow will bring, and I can tell Dante and my aunt and uncle are as well. Dante and I go for a swim in the ocean and then come back to the lounge chairs to just lie there in the sun for a while. The sun feels so good and warm on my skin. We go back and forth from the water and to the lounge chairs several times.

If it weren't for everything going on with my parents and the looming transition tomorrow, today would be the perfect day. Uncle Joe and Aunt Grace seem to be enjoying themselves as well. They picked a spot a bit farther down the beach, giving us some much-appreciated privacy. We stay on the beach until the sun starts setting.

By that time, Dante is sitting behind me on my lounge chair, and I'm relaxed back onto him, content to watch the sunset. I don't think I have ever witnessed a more beautiful sunset.

"Are you kids ready to head back?" Uncle Joe asks.

"Sure," we both say as we stand and brush off the sand from our bodies.

We grab dinner at one of the food trucks on the way out. The ride back to Dante's seems like it went by too fast. Tomorrow is coming quickly. I have to be at the Transition Center at four to start all the paperwork and such. By the time we get back to Dante's house, it's nearly ten, and we part ways to shower and head to bed.

I try to hide how nervous I am, but I know Dante sees it. I stand under the shower's hot water for a few minutes to help calm me down. It only helps a little, so I just get out, get dressed, and brush my hair and teeth. Dante waits patiently to take his shower next. He gives me a quick kiss on his way in. While he's in the bathroom, I take out the book about dark ones that Uncle Joe and Aunt Grace gave me and sit on the bed.

I'm skimming through the pages when Dante steps out with just a pair of boxers on. The look of all that sun-tanned muscle has me instantly putting the book down. He saunters over to me as slow as can be, and I can't help but stare. It's hard to believe this gorgeous man is mine. As soon as he reaches the bed, he bends down and kisses me. This isn't our typical kiss. This is a kiss full of want and need. We make out for a while until the need is too much. He makes love to me like the world is going to end. And tomorrow, it just might.

DANTE

I wake up to Sierra's head on my chest, and images from last night start running through my mind. I'm then reminded of what today is, and my heart sinks. I do want her to become like me, but I don't want her to go through all the pain it takes to do it. Her slow deep breaths fan my chest, and I gently put my arm around her without waking her. I can lie like this forever. She is everything I have ever wanted. If we can just get through today, the future will be easier.

As I am lying there watching her sleep, I make a mental note of everything we should pack for tonight. I want to make sure I can have whatever she may need. I don't want to leave her side at all tonight. She starts to stir, so I gently rub her back and brush her hair out her face with my fingers.

"Good morning, handsome," she tells me without lifting her head.

"Good morning, beautiful. How are you feeling?"

"Good, and you?" She stretches her arms above her.

"Like I am the luckiest man in the world," I answer honestly.

"I am the lucky one to have you." She lifts her head, and her eyes meet mine. After a quick kiss, she gets up and starts to dress.

"Where are you off to so fast?" I ask her.

"I need to go to the bathroom, and then I really need coffee." She rubs the sleep from her eyes.

"I now know not to get in your way until you have your coffee." I start laughing.

"Hey now, as far as I recall, you need to have coffee in the morning as well," she shoots back. I love how feisty she is.

"True. I guess I'll have to get out of bed too then."

I get dressed and follow her out into the kitchen and start making the coffee. Joe and Grace must still be sleeping. While the coffee is brewing, I begin frying some eggs in a pan for breakfast. Sierra comes up behind me and wraps her arms around me. The eggs are at a good spot, so I turn around and hug her back. Just then, Joe and Grace walk into the kitchen.

"Would you guys like some eggs?" I ask without letting Sierra go.

"That would be great, Dante. Thanks," Joe says.

"How are you feeling today Sierra? I can understand if you're nervous," Grace says.

"Good for the most part, but I just want to get it over with."

"I don't blame you. Is there anything that we can do?" Grace asks her in her motherly tone.

"No, but thanks."

The rest of the morning goes by pretty quietly. We cuddle on the couch as Sierra flips through her books. We had packed a few things she may need right after breakfast so now we were just waiting on the time to come. I packed some extra clothes, some food and my phone charger for myself. I remember going through this with my siblings, but it seems so much different now that it's her.

Sierra talks Grace into making us her famous French toast again for lunch. Once we finish eating Joe and I meet up with Gerard, leaving the girls at home. He has a contact outside of Graystone that agreed to meet with us with information on Excalibur. This meeting ends up being a dead end because the warlock who was supposed to meet us never showed.

By the time we get back to the house it's time to get going. In the truck, we try small talk to take Sierra's mind off of the transition. I hold her hand most of the ride, trying to comfort her in any way I can.

We finally arrive at the Transition Center, which is a large brick building with several pods coming off the back. Each pod is dedicated to one immortal going through the transition and their family. I park in the large parking lot and grab the duffle bag from the back. I throw the pack over my shoulder and follow Joe toward the facility. Sierra keeps biting her lower lip and isn't talking much.

We walk through the automatic doors and a friendly gentleman with a name tag that reads Roman greets us.

"What is the name that is registered?"

"Sierra Wilson, sorry Sierra Walker," Sierra says as he is looking down the list. There can be up to ten immortals going through the transition at once.

"Right this way, Ms. Walker." Roman leads the way down a long corridor. Each of the rooms on the right belong to the pods. There are numbers on the door and a medical chart hanging on the wall beside the door. "This is your pod. I will leave you to get settled and fill out the required paperwork. I will be back in about thirty minutes."

"Okay, thank you." Sierra takes the clipboard from him.

We have pod number ten at the end of the hallway. We walk in and set our bag down just on the inside of the doorway.

"Why don't you fill out the paperwork, and I can get everything unpacked," I say, trying to ease the burden on her.

"That would be great thanks, Dante."

She sits at the little round table and starts filling out all the paperwork as I grab the duffle and head toward the bedroom part of the pod. Each pod has a main bedroom, a living room with a pull-out bed, a small dinette, and a bathroom.

We had just finished unpacking and filling out the paperwork when there is a knock on the door.

"Come in," Joe says.

Roman hovers by the doorway and asks Sierra, "Are you finished with the paperwork?"

"Yes." She hands over the clipboard.

"Good. I will have you get dressed into these and come out into the hall when you are finished." Roman glances over the clipboard as if double-checking that everything is filled out.

"Okay." Sierra takes the blue ceremonial outfit from him.

"Me and your uncle will be right out in the hall," Grace says as they follow Roman from the room.

Sierra gets undressed and puts on the pants and shirt that Roman had given her. She then sweeps her long brown hair up into a ponytail and looks over at me with a smile.

"I love you, Sierra, with all my heart," I say, hoping she realizes just how much I do love her.

"And I love you with all my heart." She gives me a quick kiss.

"Are you ready?" I gaze into her beautiful hazel eyes.

"I'm as ready as I'll ever be."

We head out into the hallway where everybody has been waiting. Roman motions with a hand to follow him down another corridor, which opens out into a large round room with a ceiling made of glass. Several chairs line the wall in the back of the room for the families, while in the center of the room is a small table with all the items the Holy Ones will need to perform the ceremony, which is privately held for each immortal.

Sierra is looking around at everything in the room while Roman is explaining the process to her. They call on each immortal in the order of their room number, so Sierra will be the last transition of the night. We are directed to another waiting room down the hall while we await her turn. Each ceremony only takes about twenty minutes to complete. It looks like we will be waiting a good three hours.

I'm sure it's torture for Sierra, making us wait here throughout everybody else's ceremony. Sierra starts pacing. Then she sits down for a bit and paces some more. Finally, we are the last in the room, and she'll be called any moment now.

"Pod ten, come with me," a large burly man calls out with a deep voice.

"You got this, Sierra. I love you, and you are the strongest woman I know," I tell her, hoping she believes it.

"I love you, and you'll do great." Grace blows Sierra a kiss.

"They won't know what hit them. I love you too, and you'll kick ass." Joe winks at her.

"Thank you all, and I love you all too." She follows the large man down to the center of the room.

We take our place at the edge of the room and sit down. I can't stop bouncing my knee to try to alleviate the amount of anxiety that is in me. We watch as the Holy Ones explain to her how the ritual is performed. I never realized how scary the ceremony can look to an outsider until now. The Holy Ones, nine men and women in large hooded blue robes that reach the floor circle her. All you can see are their faces and hands.

SIERRA

There are large pillars with stones lining the room to enhance the power of the Holy Ones and to protect all of those involved. The stones include, labradorite as protection, amber to catch any negative energy, black obsidian as another protection, aqua aura for a new life, bloodstone for quick healing, serpentine to clear the chakras, moss agate to reduce pain and fear, and then amethyst to enhance the power of all the crystals.

The Holy Ones begin to chant in Italian as they take the ceremonial dagger with taaffeite gemstones imbedded throughout the handle and hold it up toward the full moon overhead. I wince in pain and clench my teeth as one of the Holy Ones cuts my left palm open and has my blood drip into a chalice held underneath by another Holy One. The chanting gets louder and faster. I can't make out what they are saying. Next, they have me kneel in front of them while another Holy One tattoos the immortal mark of a flaming sun onto the back of my neck.

The ink they use is transfused with a variety of finely ground gemstones and is only visible to others that know of this world that is hidden from the humans. Once I make the transition, complete my guardian training, and pass the evaluation, the star will be added to the inside of the sun. The star on the inside signifies that I am an immortal guardian.

Not all immortals are able to become guardians. The ones who don't usually work in town or assist the immortal guardians in some way or another. Even with all the abilities that come with being an immortal, some just are not cut out to vanquish demons and fight the dark ones. All immortal children, however, attend the Guardian Academy so they all do have some level of training. Which is something I wish I could have experienced growing up. My parents thought hiding this parallel universe from me was protecting me, but I can't help but wonder if there's more to the story than just protection.

My jaw is clenched and my body tense while they are branding me with the immortal mark. Another Holy One mixes a potion with the blood from my hand. He holds a crystal pendant above the chalice and begins a different chant. He then brings the chalice over to have me drink its contents. I swallow the bitter and metallic-tasting liquid and hand it back to the hooded figure with a weathered face. All nine Holy Ones bow their heads and hold hands in a circle around me. Then, they go silent as they all look up to the moon with closed eyes and remain still. My heart is hammering so loud in my chest I can't hear anything but my own pulse.

Finally, they step away and gesture for me to leave. I slowly walk to the back of the room on shaky legs toward my family. As soon as I'm close, Dante hugs me and I release the breath I have been holding.

"Good job baby." Dante brushes my hair away from my face.

"Thank you." I smile and turn and hug my aunt and uncle.

"You ready to get out of here?" Uncle Joe asks.

"Oh, yes." My nerves are shot and I feel jittery as if I downed several energy drinks. I hope I'm strong enough to survive this transition. I have to be, my parents are counting on me.

CHAPTER 15

SIERRA

The ceremony wasn't as bad as I thought it was going to be. The worst part was the tattoo on the back of my neck. It felt like somebody was pulling a blade across my skin repeatedly. On our way back to the pod, I'm starting to feel the effects of the transition. I knew it wouldn't take long, but I thought I had time to make it to my room before it hit me.

With each step I take, it feels like fire is running through my muscles. The pain started in my calves and worked its way up to my lower back. As soon as we step into the pod, I grab a bottle of water and sit on the edge of the bed.

"Are you doing okay?" Uncle Joe asks.

"My muscles feel like they're burning."

"Unfortunately, that's normal," Uncle Joe says with a reassuring smile.

"What can I do?" Dante is biting his lower lip and cracking his knuckles.

"I'm okay for now, just having you with me is enough," I answer. The pain is starting to get worse. My understanding is that there isn't anything I can take to help. I just have to go through it. I keep telling myself the end result will be worth it.

I grit my teeth, trying to hide how I feel. I don't want them to worry more than they already are. It's not like they can do anything anyways. I concentrate on my reasons for wanting to go through with the transition to take my mind off from the pain that is coming in waves. Dante takes out a box of cards from the nightstand.

"Do you want to play a round of crazy eights?"

"Sure," I manage to say. I know he's trying to help in whatever way he can. Maybe playing a card game might distract me. I push over on the bed, and they all get on it with me in a circle. Dante hands out the required number of cards, and we start a competitive game against each other. None of us like to lose; we found that out in the days after my parents were taken. What else could we do while we waited for news on the missing passengers.

I start getting restless from the pain. I get up and pace across the room the best I can. Every bone in my body feels like it is splintering, and I try to hide the tears. Dante immediately comes over, puts his arms around me, and holds me close. He kisses me on the top of my head.

"It's okay if it hurts, baby." He rubs my back.

"I'm sorry," I say, wiping a tear that's escaped to my cheek.

"There is nothing you have to be sorry for."

"I know it's bothering you to see me like this, and I feel bad. If you have to walk away for a little while, I'm fine with that." I can tell he's worried about me by his brows furrowing and his eyes searching mine.

"I am not going anywhere. I hate seeing you in pain, that's true, but I'll be here to help and support you in any way I can." He promises.

"I'm cold. I think I'm going to try to lie down now." A wave of cold rushes through my entire body. Another symptom of the transition taking hold of me.

By the time I get to the bed, the chills are so severe that it feels like my bones are rattling loose. Aunt Grace pulls the covers back on the bed for me to get in, and Dante helps me up onto the bed. I hadn't noticed, but Uncle Joe had turned the TV on and is asking me what I want to watch.

"I don't care. You pick," I manage to say through chattering teeth.

Dante gently climbs up into bed with me and wiggles under the covers. I've called him my heater many times, and no doubt that is what his intentions are. I try to get comfortable next to him, but the pain is too much. I end up curling up into a ball in the fetal position and can no longer fight the sobs that come. I can hear Dante saying something but I can't make out what. My heart is hammering so hard in my chest, all I hear is the blood pulsing loudly in my ear.

As my sobs get harder, it feels like another bone is breaking with every breath I take. When they said, I would feel pain like I've never felt before, they were right. I wouldn't wish this pain on my worst enemy. My eyeballs even feel like they are shattering, if that's even possible. Is it normal to have this much pain or am I going to be one of the unlucky ones who doesn't survive the transition? I can feel every cell of my body changing or dying, I'm not sure which. The last thing I recall before it all goes black is the feeling of sinking into a pit of lava with no way out.

DANTE

I thought I was prepared to be able to help Sierra through her transition, but boy was I wrong. The moment she started sobbing, I felt like there was a knife in my heart. Her sobs only grew worse as the night went on. Even though I hate it, I know this is normal. Bloodstone crystals have been placed in several different places throughout the pod to help with the healing, but the only thing that can truly help Sierra is time. I'm thankful when she finally blacks out from the pain. At least I know she won't have to endure the rest awake.

She is burning up with a fever, so I gently pull the covers back a little to leave some room for the heat to escape. Now we just wait. Some who transition can sleep for only eight hours, but others have slept for up to forty-eight hours. Her body is transforming every molecule she has into something better and stronger.

Joe hands me a silver flask filled with alcohol. The familiar burning sensation of whiskey coats my throat. I hand it back to him and nod my thanks.

"She'll pull through. We just have to give her time." Joe puts the cover back on the bottle and stashes it in his pocket.

"I know, but I didn't think it would be this hard."

I pull a chair up next to the bed and hold her hand to let her know I'm still here. For about two hours, we sit watching her small body writhe in her sleep. Then finally, she starts to calm and sleep deeply. When an immortal is going through the transition, they are almost in a state of comatose. Some have been known to be able to hear their loved ones, so I frequently tell her I love her, that she is doing great and to keep fighting. Joe and Grace do the same.

We dig out the cards again to try to distract us. We won't know if the transition is successful or not until she wakes up. If she doesn't wake up within forty-eight hours, she will not wake up at all. She'll remain in a vegetative state. I can't lose her; she is everything to me. She is my reason for breathing, my reason to get out of bed and face this relentless world. Without her, my life would have no purpose. I would have no will to live.

Joe and Grace call it a night sometime after three in the morning and retire to the pullout couch in the living room. I stay in the bedroom with Sierra. She isn't moving anymore, so I get into bed with her and lie there watching her sleep for what seems like hours. The rain pattering on the tin roof is a soothing sound, but I can't seem to fall asleep. I'm worrying too much.

Every now and then, I hear the booming sound of thunder in the distance and am reminded of how fast everything can change. The sky was cloudless when we came in. It's almost like the storm outside is also raging inside Sierra's body. Finally, too tired to go on I am able to sleep. I don't sleep well, though. I keep waking up and checking on her.

It's mid-morning, and she is still sleeping. Birds are chirping outside and the murmuring voices of Joe and Grace drift from the living room. I give Sierra a quick kiss on the forehead and head toward the sound. I go out into the living room as quietly as I can.

"Anything yet?" Joe asks me. It's been about ten hours so far.

"No, she's still sleeping."

"Keep your head up, dear. She will pull through. She's a fighter," Grace soothes.

"We stepped out to grab some donuts if you want some," Joe offers as he holds out the box to me.

My stomach is in knots. "No, thank you. I'm okay. I don't think I can eat right now."

"You should at least try. She'll need your strength when she wakes up."

"Okay, but I need coffee first."

I make my coffee in the dinette as quickly as I can and go back in the bedroom. Sierra is still lying in the same position as when I left. I sit in the chair next to the bed and hold her hand as I drink my coffee. I watch her take several slow deep breaths before I avert my eyes to my phone. I've had my phone on silent since we came in, so I'm not surprised by several missed messages.

The one that catches my eye, though, is a text from Maverick. "We need to talk. I caught a bunny." Anyone else would find the mention of a bunny confusing. But I know that it means he has intel on Excalibur. I text him back, "Sierra hasn't woken up yet. Can it wait until tomorrow?"

He texts me back almost immediately. "Yes, it can. Take care of your girl."

The rest of the messages are from random people with good wishes for Sierra or leads on pending cases not related to Excalibur. Joe and Grace come into the bedroom with a plate of donuts.

"You must eat," orders Grace.

"Yes, Ma'am," I say obediently as I reach for a chocolate glazed donut and set it on the paper plate that they offer me.

They watch and wait for me to eat, so I figure I'll make them happy and just eat the damn thing. The rain finally lets up outside, and the sun starts to peek through the clouds. I hope she wakes up soon. The wait has been agonizing. A few more hours pass with no change. I start pacing the room, not able to sit idle any longer.

I decide to step outside and get some fresh air. I sit on a little white plastic chair and try to clear my head. It's now been sixteen hours since she fell asleep. I'm panicking inside, worrying she may never wake up. I feel a strange sensation on my face, and brush my fingers across it. When they come away wet, I realize that they are tears. I haven't cried in as far back as I can remember. I never had a reason to, but now I do. I didn't hear Joe come out until he puts his hand on my back.

"It's been a hell of a past few days, hasn't it?" Joe asks.

"Yeah." I try to wipe the tears from my face.

"She's a strong one and feisty too. I don't think this world is prepared for an immortal Sierra. She will wake up soon. I can feel it." Joe tries to reassure me.

"God, I hope so," I reply, not wanting to admit that she might not.

"I got you something else while we were out. Maybe it will help take the edge off. Take all the time you need out here. We'll be right inside." Joe hands me a black flask that is full of alcohol.

"Thank you." I take a swig of whiskey. Maybe he's onto something. I won't get drunk; there's not enough in here for that. I may catch a slight buzz, and the burning of my throat is a welcome distraction. I sit outside of our pod for about ten minutes before I head back in without the fear of crying. There's nothing wrong with a man crying. I just don't want anybody to see me that vulnerable or helpless.

I go straight to the dinette and make myself another coffee, this one stronger than the last. Then I take my spot in the chair beside Sierra. I don't feel any better, but I also don't feel like a ticking time bomb ready to detonate. I'm about halfway done my coffee when I feel her fingers moving inside mine. I freeze, wanting to make sure it's not in my head before I tell the others. She does it again, just a slight movement, but it's a sign she's coming to.

"Hey, she's waking up. She's moving her fingers," I whisper to Sierra's aunt and uncle. We all hold our breath waiting to see it again.

"Do I smell coffee?" Sierra says in a hoarse and scratchy voice which doesn't resemble her own.

SIERRA

"Yeah, would you like some?" Dante asks me, sounding amused.

"Maybe water first, but then I need coffee," I say, not recognizing my own voice. My eyelids are so heavy I struggle to open them.

"Here you go, dear, it's water. I'm putting the straw on your lip." That was my Aunt Grace's voice.

With the straw in my mouth, I take a nice long drink. The cold water feels so good on my throat. I wonder how long I have been sleeping. I don't hurt anymore; I just feel stiff from the lack of movement and a little fuzzy.

"How are you feeling?" Uncle Joe asks me.

I take another drink of water before I answer, "Really tired and stiff, but other than that, I feel okay."

"That's normal, and it will wear off throughout the day."

"How long was I asleep?" Knowing it must have been hard for them.

"Almost seventeen hours," Dante answers, sounding a little hoarse himself.

"I'm sorry," I say, imagining the hell he's gone through watching me.

"Hey, it's not your fault." Dante squeezes my hand. "Good things take time."

I'm finally able to open my eyes and look around. They all look tired, especially Dante. I wonder if he got any sleep at all. The fogginess is slowly starting to lift as I drink more water. I don't feel any different than I did before the transition. I try to sit up but am overcome with lightheadedness.

"It's okay. There's no rush. You can take your time getting up. Your body has gone through hell these last twenty-four hours. Would you like me to get you some coffee?" Dante reaches out a hand to steady me.

Coffee sounds so good. "Yes please, that would be great."

"Okay, I'll be right back." Dante walks out of the room.

"Are you hungry?" Aunt Grace hovers by my shoulder.

"Yes, actually I am." The rumbling of my stomach is so loud I wouldn't be surprised if she heard it.

"What would you like to eat? They have all kinds of options in the cafeteria?" Aunt Grace takes the seat next to the bed.

I thought for a moment. "Do they have breakfast sandwiches?"

"Yes, as a matter of fact, they do. Would you like sausage or bacon?"

"Sausage please," I say as I'm slowly able to sit up straighter and put pillows behind me to lean against the hard wooden headboard.

"Anything that we can do to help, just say so," uncle Joe insists as Dante comes back into the room.

"If I would have known the smell of strong coffee was going to wake you, I would have made it sooner." Dante chuckles.

"Like my dad always says, there's nothing a strong cup of coffee can't achieve." My brain instantly reminds me of why they aren't here, and a deep sadness hits me.

"We're going to run to the cafeteria, Dante is there anything you would like?" Uncle Joe asks him.

"Sure, surprise me. I'm not picky." Dante takes the seat beside me again.

"Okay, we'll be back." They head out toward the door.

"You're looking a little better." Dante hands me the coffee.

"Well, I feel a lot better." I take a sip of coffee. It's hot on my throat, but it tastes so good.

"I'm so grateful you're awake and recovering." Dante leans in and kisses me on the forehead.

"So, what happens now?"

"Well, there is a celebration tomorrow night in honor of those who went through the transition these last few days. Usually, there's a week off and then a few months of more training to prepare you for the actual guardian qualification. But I'm not sure with you since you didn't attend the Guardian Academy in the first place."

"So, the week off, I can do whatever I want?" I raise my eyebrows.

"Within reason, yes." His expression turns wary.

"Okay, good," I say, not wanting to explain just yet. I want to help find my parents in whatever way I can.

"It sounds like you're scheming." Dante cocks his head to the side.

"When do you think we can get out of here?" I change the subject.

"Well, that depends on when you are able to be up moving around safely."

"Room service." Uncle Joe knocks on the door.

"Come in." I like the thought of being able to eat.

We all eat in relative quiet, and I start feeling much better as I'm able to get up and go to the bathroom without feeling dizzy. We're able to check out soon after and head back to Dante's house. We take it easy for the rest of the day by lounging around, watching movies, and eating popcorn. Tomorrow will be a new day. I am hoping to talk to the High Council again about my parents. Something needs to be done, and I'm not going to wait around any longer.

CHAPTER 16

SIERRA

I talked to Gabriel, the cleric to the High Council earlier in the morning and he said he would talk to the Master Council and let me know what I was supposed to do next. I'm feeling a lot better today, at least. I still don't notice any changes within me from the transition. Tonight, we're going to the Transition Celebration, which celebrates our rebirth into something magnificent. The High Council will be there as well as immortals, witches, and warlocks who belong to the high society. All of the immortals who transitioned with me, as well as their families, will be present too.

Dante said that there would be a presentation followed up by a meal then a ball. I've never been to a ball before, but he told me it's pretty much like a high school prom. I'm excited to be able to wear that beautiful dress he gave me. Shortly after breakfast, I hear back from Gabriel.

"Hello Ms. Walker, the Master Council wants me to inform you that you are expected to be at the Guardian Academy next Monday morning at eight sharp. There they will assess what you will need for education or training, and that will guide them into a plan for you. I would suggest you take this coming week to go over to the library and gain as much knowledge as you can."

"Great, thank you for your time, Gabriel," I reply, then hang up.

I hope I can talk Dante into letting me visit Emma. I've only talked to her once since the plane crash. We've never gone this long without speaking before. I use the rest of the day to flip through the books that Aunt Grace and Uncle Joe gave me and try to gather as much information as I can in as little time as I can.

Before I know it, it's time to get ready for the Transition Celebration. Once showered, I decide to wear my long wavy brown hair down. I clip the very top of my hair back so it will stay out of my face with a small silver barrette with white pearls decorating the top. I use a small amount of concealer to even out my skin tone and follow up with some light brown eyeshadow and black eyeliner.

I pull the bohemian style dress off the hanger, step into it, and I pulled it up over my hips. There is no zipper or snaps; it has an elastic waistband on the inside to give it that fitted look. Dante did an amazing job picking this dress out, and it fits my curves perfectly. I look in the mirror and think of how much my life has changed since my eighteenth birthday. I wish my parents were here. I don't know why it's taking the investigative team so long to find my parents and Excalibur. I hope my mom and dad would be proud of the woman I'm becoming.

I step out of the bathroom, and Dante is already dressed sitting in the small chair in the corner of the bedroom. As soon as I walk out of the bathroom, he stands up and eyes me from head to toe.

"Wow, babe, you look so gorgeous." He walks over and puts his hands on my waist.

"You look very handsome. I could get used to seeing you in a suit." He's wearing a black suit jacket with matching black pants, a white dress shirt, and a green silk tie. I have never seen a man look this good in a suit before.

"I might have to take you out and show you off more often." He bends down for a kiss.

The kiss ends too soon as usual since we had to leave shortly to make it there in time. After I slip on my white shoes, I stand up and spin around in a circle.

"What do you think?"

"That you will be the most beautiful woman to ever walk through those ballroom doors." Dante stares at me with a smile I've never seen on him before.

"Oh, stop it. You're the one all the other ladies will be ogling." I grin back at him.

"I guess you better keep me close then, just in case," he goads, playing along.

"I might just have to do that." Smiling, I tweak his nose.

I love the way he makes me feel. He makes me feel happy, worthy, and beautiful but most importantly, loved without condition. He has always supported me and loved me even if I wasn't aware. He really is my soul mate, my twin flame, my anima gemella. We walk out of our bedroom and meet Uncle Joe in the kitchen. He too is wearing a black suit, but his tie is a light purple color.

"Wow, you clean up nice, Uncle Joe," I say with my hands on my hips.

"I could say the same about you. It's not often you wear a dress." He eyes me with raised brows.

"Maybe I wasn't given a good enough reason to want to wear one," I say as an excuse. Just then, Aunt Grace comes around the corner wearing a pretty light purple maxi dress with cap sleeves that matches uncle Joe's tie.

"You look beautiful, Aunt Grace."

"Same with you, Sierra." Aunt Grace's warm smile and twinkling eyes make her look younger than she is.

"Are we ready to head out?" Dante asks everyone.

"Yes." We all say as Dante takes out his blue benitoite stone from his pocket and creates a portal to the town square.

From the other side of the tunnel, I recognize the large round water fountain in the center. I step through and the others follow. Dante's best friend Maverick and his girlfriend Vivian are waiting for us by the fountain. Dante introduces us all to each other. He has told me quite a bit about Maverick, and from the sounds of it, Maverick is Dante's Emma.

Dante takes me by the hand as we walk along the cobblestone sidewalk toward the hall that holds the ball. I know we reach the venue when we get to a large white marble building with six large round pillars in the front. There is a wide staircase leading up to the entrance with a line of about twenty or so people waiting to get in. The line moves fairly quickly, and we reach the base of the steps within ten minutes.

"The name of your party?" the doorman asks.

"Sierra Walker," I answer. That name still seems foreign to me.

"And how many in your party?"

"Six total."

"Welcome to the ball." He waves his hand toward the door.

As we walk up the marble steps, I can't help but remember Emma's theory about me being a royal. If only she could see me now dressed like a princess and headed to a ball. It's customary to sign the guest list when you arrive and pose with your partner for a picture prior to gaining access to the ballroom. I will have to see how we can get a copy of the picture, because the way Dante looks tonight is not an image I would ever like to forget.

We make it through the crowd of people to some tables that have been set up on one half of the giant room. Dante pulls a chair out for me, and I sit along with the rest of our group. I have never been in a place this fancy before. As I look around the room there are carved arches above each of the large windows with the curtains tied back and many chandeliers hanging from the ceiling, which has intricate patterns carved into it as well. The floor has a shiny checkerboard design with a cream color like the walls and a brownish shade like the curtains that are tied back.

Once everybody inside finds a seat at a table, an elegant-looking woman in a light blue dress takes the podium at the front of all the tables.

"Hello everyone, and welcome to this celebration of life. We will be celebrating those who have been reborn into an eternal being of a higher purpose. My name is Adelaide, and I will be your host for this evening. As many of you are aware, one of our young immortals did not survive the transition. Let us bow our heads and pray that Dion has safe passage to those who have fallen before him." She bows her head in silence.

I didn't know one of them didn't make it; nobody said anything to me. I knew there was a slight risk I may not survive, but I really didn't think much about others who have trained their whole lives for it. I bow my head in silence and wonder why I was able to make it and not him. Dante must sense I'm upset because he reaches over and gives my knee a squeeze.

The woman at the podium continues, "To go through the transition and become your true self is to accept the duty that comes along with the gift. Your duty can involve becoming an immortal guardian to keep the balance of good and evil in the world or it can involve residing in Graystone and working for our community. You are all equally important. Without one, we could not have the other. Life is about balance, after all, and you, my young immortals, are what holds the key to the success of our future. You have all worked hard to reach where you are today, and that, my friends, is worth celebrating."

She finishes with a curtsey and walks away from the podium as waitresses and waiters come around the tables with drinks and trays of finger food.

We eat so many different appetizers, I'm afraid my dress will not fit me by the end of the night. It doesn't help that they offer wine on top of it. I've never drank wine before tonight, so I tried a few types that they bring around. I quickly realize I am not a dry wine type of girl. I like the sweetness of the Moscato they offer. Once our party is done having their fill of all the tasty food, we try out the dance floor on the opposite side of the ballroom.

There is soft instrumental music playing throughout the room, but it's louder on the dance floor side. Dante and I dance for what seems like hours. As he spins me around on the dancefloor and holds me close, everybody else fades away until it's just us. When I look into his eyes and he smiles that charming smile, nothing else matters.

There are no bad guys; my parents haven't been abducted, I wouldn't have to leave Emma behind. If only it could stay like this for forever.

"I'm sorry, but I have to use the restroom," I say, regretting all the wine I drank.

"Me too. I'll walk you there." He escorts me to the lady's room. He's always such a gentleman.

We part ways to both use the restrooms, and I can't believe the sheer amount of details in the bathrooms. The walls and ceiling were just as intricately designed as the rest of the building. They didn't skimp on anything. Even the toilets look high class if there is such a thing. Dante is already waiting for me when I step out of the restroom. Maverick is there as well with Vivian.

"Hey babe, Maverick and I are going to step outside for a moment. Will you be okay with Vivian for a few minutes?" Dante asks me.

"Of course. Take your time. It'll be good for me to hear some dirt on you anyway," I joke.

"Oh really, is that how this is?" He pulls me in for a kiss.

"Well, in my defense, you do kind of already know most of the dirt on me," I say in between kisses.

"That is true," Maverick interjects on my behalf.

"Thank you, Maverick," I say.

"Hey, you're supposed to be on my side." Dante jabs him in the ribs.

"I am. I just agreed that she was telling the truth," he says, defending himself.

"Okay, we'll be right back." Dante and Maverick stride away toward the back exit.

I walk back to the table we have been occupying with Vivian and we each take a seat. "Thank you for coming tonight, Vivian."

"You're welcome. It's nice to get Maverick dressed up from time to time," she says wistfully.

"They do look good all dressed up, don't they?"

"Yes, they do," she says, and we both start giggling.

I watch Uncle Joe and Aunt Grace on the dancefloor and they seem to be enjoying themselves. Vivian and I talk back and forth for a while about so many subjects. She did not, however, divulge any dirt on Dante as I had hoped. The guys are gone for so long that we start to worry and decide to find them. I want to get in a few more dances before they shut it down. We head out of the ballroom and toward the exit at the back of the building that both buys had disappeared through.

We step through a pair of double doors and out onto a stone walkway. It's peaceful out here, much quieter than inside. I catch sight of a small gazebo off to the right and half expected them to be there but no such luck. We then follow a narrow trail leading into the woods. They must have sensed us coming because they step out of the woods at that moment. I wonder what they were doing in the forest?

DANTE

Maverick and I are walking on the small pathway leading into the woods. There are a few others outside getting fresh air as well, so if we want to talk freely, the dense trees would give us privacy.

Maverick clears his throat, "Look, I don't know how else to tell you this, but the High Council is pulling the plug on the investigation of Excalibur and the search for Sierra's parents."

"What?" My jaw clenches. I'm hoping I heard that wrong.

"Justina told me earlier today that the High Council claims they've exhausted all of their resources and there's been no new information coming to light." Maverick shakes his head back and forth.

"It's only been two weeks. They have an unlimited amount of resources they can tap into." I search the area around us to make sure we are still alone.

"I know, I don't understand it either. The High Council has spent more resources and time on enemies that pose less of a threat." Maverick's nostrils are flaring.

"What is wrong with them? We can't just abandon Sierra's parents or the others that have been taken. There's no telling what Excalibur will do next if he continues to get away with kidnapping immortals and taking down planes full of innocent bystanders." I pace in the small clearing we're standing in.

I can't go back to Sierra like this, I need to calm down first. I trample the same path over and over again, taking my anger out on the unsuspecting ground below me. How can the High Council cancel the investigation? Or more importantly why would they stop looking for Excalibur so fast? When I'm convinced I can walk back into the ballroom without ripping the heads off from the councilmen's bodies, Maverick and I head toward the building silently. Just as we reach the edge of the woods, we spot Sierra and Vivian.

"Hey, ladies," Maverick says sauntering toward his girlfriend.

"Hey, yourself." Vivian wraps her arms around Maverick.

"Sierra, will you come take a walk with me?" I try to hide my dismay.

"Sure," Sierra says, searching my face.

Maverick and Vivian head back into the structure. Sierra has to hold her dress up with both hands so it won't drag on the ground. Maybe if I had gotten her taller heels, it wouldn't drag? But then again, she probably wouldn't have worn the taller ones anyway. I gesture for her to go in front of me, and so she does.

The sight of her walking through the woods seems almost magical with the ground covered in fallen leaves, the moon and twinkling stars casting her in a glow of their own making. She looks over her shoulder at me and gives me one of her dazzling smiles. Seeing that look only reconfirms that she is everything to me. She may be my anima gemelli, but I just now realize she is the sun that my world revolves around.

How can I tell her what Maverick just told me? How can I break her heart? We knew there was a possibility that the High Council was compromised. I didn't want to believe that could happen, but it has. She looks so happy tonight, and I don't want to ruin it. The bad news can wait until morning. I want her to have this one night of happiness. We reach a small circular clearing in the woods with wrought iron benches around the perimeter. She takes a seat at one of them and I sit beside her.

"I found something that made me think of you. Let me see your hand." I pull the bracelet out of my pocket I had bought her a few days ago. I gently wrap it around her small wrist and close the clasp.

"Awe, Dante it's beautiful." She turns her wrist back and forth and smiles at the seashell charms.

"When we have time off, there are other beaches I would love to bring you to." I'm trying to bite down my anger and not let it show.

"I would like that very much."

"So how much dirt did Vivian dish on me?" I ask her.

"Actually, none. She said there wasn't any dirt to give." Sierra sounds amused.

"Oh, thank god. I owe her one," I say dramatically brushing my forehead and enjoying how the act makes her giggle. I haven't heard much of that in a while. She has a laughter that is contagious. She could walk in any room and make people feel joy; she just has that personality. That's why it's so hard to see her sad or upset as she has been lately.

"We should probably get back in there. I would like to dance to a few more songs with you. If you're up for it?" Sierra gazes into my eyes.

"To dance with a smart and beautiful woman such as yourself? I wouldn't dream of passing that up." We both got up off the bench and head back.

We dance to a few more songs before the transition ceremony ends. We say our goodbyes to Vivian and Maverick with the hopes of doing a double date soon and catch up to Joe and Grace.

"Are you guys heading back to my place?" I ask them.

"We will in a little while. There's some things I'd like to show Grace." Joe looks lovingly at his wife.

"Okay, we'll see you later then. Thank you for coming tonight." Sierra gives them both a hug.

"We wouldn't miss it." Grace squeezes her niece.

We use a portal to get to my place, and I'm excited to have the house to ourselves for a little while. I enjoy having her family around, and I know she does too. But there's not much privacy when others are here, so it'll be nice to have an evening just for us. With everything going on in the past two weeks, we really haven't had a first date. I have tonight planned out already. I just need the time to be able to set it all up. I want it to be perfect for her, she deserves that. I need her to have something good to hold onto. Tomorrow when I tell her that the High Council is putting her parents lives at risk, I don't know how she will take the news.

CHAPTER 17

DANTE

I never heard Joe and Grace come in last night, and I hope they made it back in. I gave them my spare key just in case. I want them here when I tell Sierra that the High Council called off the investigation of her parent's disappearance. She may need them for support. I don't think it will go well, which is understandable. Given the severity of the situation and possible implications, I am at a loss for what I should do.

Sierra is sleeping with her head on my chest as I'm trying to find the best way to tell them. I have been awake for a while now. I didn't get much sleep last night thinking about it. I don't want to cause Sierra any pain, but she needs to know the truth. It was really hard keeping it from her last night. I can hear what sounds like dishes clanging, so Joe and Grace must be here. That's kind of a relief. At least Joe can probably help me figure this out. Sierra starts moving slightly, so I hold my breath, not ready for the day. She lifts her head, and her eyes meet mine.

"Good morning, handsome." She stretches against me and rubs her eyes.

"Good morning, beautiful," I reply as she starts making her way off the bed to get dressed. "Running away from me so fast?"

"Yes, I am. I'd like to go into town this morning and check out some of the shops. Would you like to go with me?" Sierra asks me. It's been really hard on her to be patient with the investigation.

"Yes, I would."

I get out of bed and dress. She will probably change her mind about wanting to hit up the shops after I tell her about her parents. I follow her out to the kitchen, and I can hear the coffee pot brewing already.

"Would you guys like some muffins we picked them up on the way back last night?" Grace holds out a bakery box.

"Yes ma'am, I love muffins." I reach into the box and pull a blueberry flavored one out, my favorite.

"Me too," Sierra agrees.

"Why don't you sit? I'll get the coffee." I pull out a chair for Sierra to take a seat next to Grace who's sipping her water.

"Okay, thank you."

I grab two red mugs from the cupboard since Joe and Grace already have theirs on the counter. The coffee pot finishes brewing as I gather the creamer and sugar and set them on the kitchen table. I pour all four red mugs full of coffee and bring them as well. We eat our muffins and drink our coffee in relative quiet as my dread keeps growing. I wait until everybody finishes before I deliver the news.

"I was told last night the High Council called off the investigation into Excalibur and the plane crash. The investigative team was told to stand down by the Master Council." I take a glance at Sierra but her face went blank.

"You have got to be kidding me. Why?" Joe asks, his face flushing a dark red.

"According to my source, they were using too much manpower and money to try to find somebody who is a ghost." I meet his furious gaze.

"So, they're just giving up?" Sierra looks at me, and I can see the hurt in her eyes.

"Unfortunately, that's what it looks like," I answer honestly, hating the fact that I'm the one causing her pain right now.

"What about my parents?" Sierra's voice is very quiet as she stares down at her hands.

I have always been taught that honesty is the best way, no matter how blunt. "Since your parents aren't immortal guardians anymore, the investigators can't be forced to do a search and rescue. That's how the High Council is getting away with not looking for Michael and Sophia."

"How are we going to get my parents back then?"

"I don't know, babe, I really don't. Joe, do you have any thoughts?" I ask as I reach for Sierra's hand. I can see the tears forming in her eyes even though she won't lift her head up.

"Ah!" Grace yelps, and we all look toward her as a sphere of what looked like water crashes onto the table.

"That wasn't me." Joe gets up to grab the towel hanging off the stove.

"Me either," I say as we all look to Sierra.

"Well, it wasn't me. I don't know how to do any of that." Sierra frowns at us all.

"It definitely wasn't me, although it came out of my glass." Grace laughs while trying to dry herself off with the towel.

"Sierra, what were you thinking about just now?" Joe asks as he refills Grace's glass of water.

"I was thinking about how this is all so messed up. My parents wouldn't be in this position if the High Council would've done their damn job in the first place." Sierra folds her arms against her chest and lifts her chin.

"I get that. That's how we all feel. Focus that feeling on this glass of water," Joe directs her.

"It's not doing anything. I told you it wasn't me." She frowns at the glass of water.

"It's okay, just keep trying. Think about your parents," Joe says as we are all watching intently. Then the water starts to ripple on top.

"That a girl! Keep going," Grace says.

The water, ever so slowly, rises from the glass. Then it falls back into the cup. At least this time Grace doesn't wear it.

"Great job Sierra!" I tell her as proudly as I can. Too bad it took such a crappy situation to bring her gift out.

"I think we should bring this party outside before we trash Dante's house," Joe says, trying to lighten the mood.

On the way to the back deck, Joe grabs a large bowl full of water. I've never actually seen an elemental gift before in an immortal. The fairies can manipulate plants and trees. It seems Joe has some experience in guiding the newly gifted.

"This won't help find my parents. I would rather focus my energy on that," Sierra insists.

"Well, from the sounds of it, dear, we will be the only ones looking for them. Your gifts, however new they are, may play a role in helping." Grace's eyes and smile warm with kindness.

"I think you're on to something, Grace. What if we put together our own team to try to locate them?" I ask the question before I think it through. That would mean going against the High Council and can be punishable by law.

"What other option do we have?" Joe says my next thought out loud.

"We will have to compile a list of potential allies we can trust." I'm already thinking of a few.

"I may know of some other immortals who can help, also we have a friend who's a witch that no longer pledge's her allegiance with the High Council. Konstantina was able to help our family when we left Graystone, we can trust her. Are you sure you understand what you are risking by helping us?" Joe asks me pointedly.

"Yes, I do. And I'm in one hundred percent. I also know of a warlock who may be able to assist us." I have to help Sierra. There's no other option.

"Well, kid, it looks like you're getting a crash course on how to use your gift." Joe pats his niece on the back.

A steely look enters Sierra's eyes. "If it will help get my parents back, I'm up for it."

SIERRA

The gravity of how desperate we are is finally starting to sink in. Dante left a few hours ago to talk face-to-face with some potential immortals that could help us. Uncle Joe has been trying to help me use my gift, but it's very uncontrollable right now. Sometimes I'm able to manipulate the water, but not often. My emotions are all over the place which probably isn't helping. I keep trying hard to concentrate on what I want to do, but the water doesn't seem to want to cooperate. I am furious with the High Council for dropping the investigation; they're just abandoning my parents. For every good thing that happens, something twice as bad happens next.

Uncle Joe thinks it's a good idea once Dante comes back to pack up and leave Graystone. I thought I could be really happy here, but it doesn't look like that will work out. Maybe if we can assemble a force big enough to take down Excalibur, we can break the glamour on the High Council. If that's even what it is. Who's to say they aren't working together willingly? I hate for Dante to have to leave his home, but I understand where Uncle Joe is coming from. My parent's enemies could be watching us and anticipating our next move.

I hate the fact that Dante could lose his immortal guardian status because of me and my family. It's just so unfair. I did manage to create what Uncle Joe coined a water bomb and throw it a few feet from me, so that's some progress. I'm not sure how hydrokinesis will be effective against Excalibur, but Uncle Joe seems to think it will be. Aunt Grace is inside baking up a storm. She only bakes like this when she's stressed out. Aunt Grace claims she's making this much food to take with us, but Uncle Joe and I know the real reason. She's scared.

We decide to give training a break and start making a list of supplies that we may need such as weapons, food, clothing and other gear. Later in the day, Dante finally comes back and looks like he's been through hell.

"Well, I managed to get a few people to join. There are a couple of others who are on the fence, though." Dante takes a seat at the kitchen table.

"It's a good starting point. Baby Poseidon here was able to make a water bomb," Uncle Joe says proudly. I'll let the nickname go for now.

"Really? That's awesome. Good job, babe!" Dante beams at me.

"Thanks."

"So, I had a thought I would like to run by you," Uncle Joe says to Dante.

"Shoot."

"If we're going to do this under the radar, the best thing to do would be to gather any supplies we could possibly need and leave Graystone."

"That's what I thought as well. That's part of why it took me so long. A few of the guys said they would chip in toward a secure base of operations, and I think we found the perfect place. There is a private island in the Caribbean with a medieval stone keep castle in immaculate condition. If we could get a few warlocks or witches to enact a force field around it, the island could be impenetrable. There are close to two hundred acres, so we would have plenty of space for others who will join us and plenty of room to train," Dante explains.

"I think that's a great idea." Uncle Joe leans a hip against the kitchen counter.

"Would you like to come with me to check it out first?" Dante leans back in his chair.

"No, I trust your judgment. If you say it will be safe for us, then it will be. I'll pitch in as well," Uncle Joe agrees.

"Wait, are we really moving to a castle? In the Caribbean? You can afford that?" I know it may sound rude, but I can't help asking.

"It looks like that would be the safest way. Strategically it makes the most sense, and yes most of us immortal guardians have money. After living for hundreds of years you run out of things to spend it on," Dante says with a smirk.

"When can we go?" I don't even to try to hide my excitement. I have never been to the Caribbean before but have always wanted to.

"As soon as we can all get packed and head into town. It probably would be best to split up and each hit different stores with a list of supplies to gather and then be on our way," Uncle Joe says.

Dante's expression grows serious. "Okay, I will go make sure the purchase of the property goes smoothly." Dante takes out his phone and heads out onto the back lawn.

After some debating about things we could need and what we can buy elsewhere such as food, we each have a long list of items to get from town. I'm ecstatic about the items I need to buy at the alchemy shop. Aunt Grace has the task of gathering kitchen equipment that Dante does not already have in his home. Since Aunt Grace and I are unable to create a portal, we need to meet up with one of the guys when we finish buying everything on our list. When we portal into the town square, it's a little bittersweet. I was really looking forward to living here.

We each have a burner cell phone that Dante picked up before coming back to Graystone. Once I am in the alchemy shop, I load up my shopping basket with the vials of chemical compounds as well as some herbs and flowers. Dante said he had a stockpile already of elixirs and some other stuff, but it wouldn't hurt to pick up more, so I grab some extras. I also add a blue benitoite portal stone and a large collection of crystals and gemstones to my cart. I get quite the eyeballs from the shopkeeper when I reach to the counter with my overflowing basket.

"Going all out, are we?" The old man arches a bushy eyebrow.

"Well, it's all new to me, so I figured this was the best way for me to learn."

"By all means, don't let me stop you."

I pay with my debit card. I guess it's a good thing I saved a lot of my money. After I step out of the store with two full bags, I send Dante a text letting him know I'm ready. For now, we are stashing things at his house until we have it all. All too soon the High Council will figure out what we're doing, so we are on a tight clock. Once we are all back to Dante's with our arsenal of supplies, we start packing them into empty duffle bags and suitcases to make the trip a little easier.

Dante creates a portal to the compound and as soon as we step though we look up in awe at the sheer size of the castle. It has to be at least three stories high at the lowest point. I can smell the salty ocean breeze from nearby, but unfortunately, I can't see the ocean from where I stand.

We grab our suitcases and duffle bags and enter through the large wooden door with reinforced iron bars. I'm not even a little surprised to see Maverick here, adding his duffle bag to the pile of others near the front entrance, but there isn't any sign of Vivian.

"How do you want to do this?" Maverick asks Dante.

"I think whoever shows up can just pick a bedroom. There are plenty in here, and if we run out, we'll think of something." Dante adjusts the strap to his pack on his shoulder.

"Sounds good. We should just get unpacked and settled in for tonight, and we'll start planning tomorrow." Uncle Joe reaches for another bag.

"All right with me," Dante replies.

We grab as much as we can from the pile of bags from the numerous trips and move down the long corridor toward some of the bedrooms. The rest of the people separate from us and choose their own bedrooms nearby. I'm surprised that we have eight others who are willing to risk their lives or jail time to help us eliminate Excalibur and find all the missing immortals. I wasn't all that surprised when Dante had told us that there were others taken after my parents. Dante and I stop about halfway down the hall in front of a bedroom to the right.

"Does this look okay to you?" Dante raises his eyebrows and peeks into the room.

"As long as I'm with you, any of them will be good," I answer him as Uncle Joe and Aunt Grace move farther down the hallway.

The room's fairly large with a king size bed and a table set in front of a fireplace. I'm happy to see modern amenities such as electric lights and plugins. We put our bags down and go back to the front of the building for the rest of our belongings. Once we're finally able to stay in our room and unpack our bags we're able to relax a little. As I'm putting my clothing in the bureau, I realize that we didn't stock the kitchen. We'll have to go elsewhere for food.

"How are you holding up?" Dante leans his back against the worn wooden dresser. "You look a bit tired."

"I'm okay. I just want to get my parents back safely. That is, if they're still alive." I blink back tears.

"I'm going to try to visit one of them in a dream again tonight. I haven't had any luck so far, but it's worth a shot." Dante gently brushes away the tear that managed to escape my left eye.

"That would be wonderful if you could." I drop down on the edge of the bed. "I don't know where I'd be if it weren't for you. I'm sorry you had to leave Graystone. I know you loved it there."

"I did love Graystone, but I love you more. If this is the path that you need to go on, I'll follow you anywhere," he says, sitting down beside me and wrapping me in a hug.

"I love you too," I say before getting interrupted by a knock at the door.

Uncle Joe opens it and stands in the threshold. "Hey kids, I was able to reach Konstantina. She said she'll need another witch or warlock to be able to create a barrier around the island. Were you able to touch base with your warlock friend?"

"I was. Reid will be here by the morning. He had some things to take care of first," Dante replies.

"That's good. It looks like this team of justice seekers is coming together nicely," Uncle Joe says sounding a little surprised himself.

"Not bad for short notice. We'll have to send somebody for groceries soon." Dante rubs his arm.

"Yeah, I figured we would. Grace is in the pantry seeing what we'll need for food. She volunteered to keep all of us fed, poor woman. I don't think she knows what she just got herself into." Uncle Joe shakes his head and laughs.

"I bet she didn't. Although, I can't think of somebody who would be better at it." I think Aunt Grace is where I get my love of food from.

CHAPTER 18

DANTE

Sierra is out on the lawn practicing her gift with some of the others trying to guide her. Besides the four of us, we have six immortals, one witch, and one warlock. It's not enough, but it's a good start. I never would have seen myself going against the High Council if it wasn't for Sierra. I would do anything to keep her safe. Something doesn't feel right about the High Council. I'm hoping that their minds are being controlled by Excalibur. Because if that isn't the case, then that means they're dangerous and not to be trusted.

Once everybody's settled in for the night, I try to reach Michael or Sophia through the dream realm. Again, I find nothing. Something or someone must be blocking them from me. Since their abduction, I've been trying to reach them at least once a day. Trying to contact them tonight is exhausting, and I find myself falling asleep almost before my head hits the pillow.

I wake up in the morning by Sierra's soft voice. "Hey, handsome. It's time to get moving."

"I don't want to, though," I say, acting like a child.

"But you have to. Come on, get up, sleepyhead," she orders, poking me in the side just below my ribs.

"Why?" I stretch my arms over my head. "The bed is so warm."

"Because Reid is here, and he wants to talk to you."

I groan and mutter, "Then I guess if I have to."

"You do," she says, laughing. "He's in the great hall."

Once showered and dressed, I head to meet Reid. I met Konstantina last night, and I think they'll make a good team to shield our island. I met Reid several years ago through Maverick. He doesn't have an allegiance with the High Council, only because he likes to help humans with mostly harmless magic. He does not harm them and believes in all the rest of our laws besides having to hide from humans what he is.

"Well, look what the cat dragged in. Did you enjoy your beauty sleep?" Reid asks. He saunters over to me. His black hair hits below his shoulders, and he has a nervous habit of twirling the strands when no one is looking.

"I did, actually. It looks like you could use some as well. Emphasis on the beauty part," I shoot back as we both start laughing.

Reid pulls me in for a quick hug. "It is good to see you my friend, minus the circumstances of course."

"It's good to see you too, and thank you for coming. We can use all the help we can get," I say honestly.

"I wondered if there would come a time that the High Council would be compromised." Reid glances around the large empty hall that's echoing our voices.

"Well, we don't know that for sure yet. They could be having their minds controlled by Excalibur." I don't want to believe that they would voluntarily do something to Sierra's parents.

"We can hope. Where is this lovely Konstantina I'm tasked with helping?" He pats down the lapels of his suit jacket.

"Konstantina will be down in a minute," I say, and it's as if she heard us because at that moment she walks into the great hall. The heels of her blue stilettos clicking along.

"Hello again, Dante." Konstantina's curly dark blue hair stands out in contrast to the white dress she is wearing.

"Good morning, Konstantina. This is my friend Reid I was telling you about."

"You didn't mention how dashing your friend is," she says, checking out Reid.

"And he failed to mention how stunning you are, my lady." Reid kisses the top of her hand.

"Anyway, we were hoping that between the two of you, you could create a magical shield over the island like the one around Graystone?" I ask them.

"I believe we can manage that. I'm assuming you only want to allow select people here?" Reid asks.

"If that's possible."

"I think if we can tie the magic to azurite stones, that will allow the carrier of the stone to pass through. What do you think?" Konstantina flashes a smile at Reid.

"I think that would work. How many do you want to allow?" Reid asks, looking toward me.

"Well, currently, we have twelve, but I am hoping more will join. I'm thinking maybe around thirty?"

"How about we cast a larger spell to enchant several stones, and then we can have them on hand if you're able to get others to join?" As Konstantina talks it's hard not to notice Reid staring at her and tapping the side of his face with a finger.

I know we picked the right witch and warlock for the job. "That sounds like a good idea to me. Thank you both, and let me know if you need anything."

"I will do that," Reid says.

"Let's get to work." Konstantina clasps her hands together in front of her.

I go back to our bedroom, thinking Sierra will be there, but she isn't. I send her a quick text to see where she is and find out she's helping Grace in the kitchen.

When I enter the large kitchen full of cupboards and counters, I ask, "What can I help with?"

"If you can round everybody up, breakfast will be done in about ten minutes," Grace says.

"I can do that." I give Sierra a quick kiss on the cheek and head back out.

Everyone makes it to the dining room just in time for the women to bring out the breakfast. The scent of warm bread teases my nose. They insist on serving us some sort of breakfast casserole with eggs, veggies, and cheese with a side of apple cinnamon bread.

Once we finish eating our breakfast, we start brainstorming what we know of Excalibur which really isn't much. By midafternoon Konstantina and Reid manage to create the shield over the island. Having a barrier that will block unauthorized visitors makes me feel a lot better about our safety. I felt exposed last night, and I didn't like that at all. I decide I would try to catch Sierra's parents again even though it's only three here.

I quickly create a simple dream of Michael and Sophia's house. It is a good thing I do because I'm able to get a bead on Michael. When I find a faint glimmer of his thoughts, I focus harder. Once I finally lock onto his subconscious, I'm able to dig further until I reach his conscious mind. He looks shocked that I'm in his house. If it was under other circumstances, I would find his reaction funny.

"Hi, Michael, you're probably aware this is a dream, but it's far more than that. I'm able to communicate with you as a dreamwalker," I say, so he understands what is going on.

His gaze widens in shock. "Well, that makes perfect sense now. How is Sierra? Is she okay?"

"Yes, but she's very worried about you guys."

"Oh, thank God, when I saw her name on that list, I thought the worst."

Having her name on a list can't be good news. "What do you mean you saw her name?"

"Well, you won't believe this, but Emma's parents are working with Excalibur."

My stomach grows cold as ice. "Is Emma involved as well?" I dare to ask. If she is that will crush Sierra.

"According to Eric, he said she knows nothing. They're cataloging us on a spreadsheet by our gifts."

My eyes widen. "You've talked to Eric? I knew I didn't like him. There was always something about that guy I didn't trust." I have to clench my fists to keep my anger in check.

"Yes, but I think we can trust him. He admitted that he's being blackmailed into doing things for Raymond and his boss, which I'm assuming is Excalibur. They're using Emma as leverage to get Eric to do what they want."

"And why do you think we can trust him?"

"Well, he did give me some pills that would help cancel out the iron's power that we are bound by. I know that they work because my gift of seeing the future has come back," Michael says.

"What kind of vision did you have this time?" I sit on the brown cushion of the living room couch.

"It was about Sierra going through the transition." Michael sits beside me.

"I hate to be the one to tell you this, but she did already go through the transition. I swear it was all her decision," I tell him.

"Well, I'll be damned. How was it?"

"She's doing fine." I don't want to go into details because just thinking of Sierra's pain and what she went through gets me upset, and we don't have time for that right now. "We can catch up later once we get you guys back. Do you know where you are?"

"I believe we're in India somewhere because I overheard one of the guards talking about Nicobar Island," he answers.

"Okay, that helps. Is there anything else that you can tell me?"

"They've been drawing our blood daily since we've been abducted. It's always by Charlotte, Emma's mother. We've tried to talk to her, but she doesn't say anything besides what's necessary to draw our blood. We're being held in the basement of a stone building. I am in an east-facing cell. There are a few other prisoners down here as well. We are all in our own cells, and I know at least Sophia and I are bound in iron. I'm not sure about the others. A guard named Theodore might be the weakest link. He gives us extra food and water and has been nicer than the others, so he may be able to help," Michael says running a hand through his disheveled dirty blonde hair.

"Okay, that's good, that will help. You should know the High Council dropped the investigation of your disappearance, and we believe that they're having their minds controlled by Excalibur." Seeing the deeper lines of exhaustion around his mouth and by his eyes makes me want to reassure him. "We have assembled a small team so far and we're going to try to get the both of you out of there. Is there anybody that you know that could help us?"

"You're going against the High Council?" He stares back at me in disbelief. "That's pretty daring."

"Yes, and I am aware of what that means. Do you know anybody who would take that risk as well?"

"Besides Joe, we have a friend who's a witch who may help. Her name is Konstantina. Eric would probably help if he knows Emma would be safe."

"We have a secure compound, and we already have Konstantina on board. I will see what I can do about Emma. Are you really sure we can trust him, though?" I ask, not really wanting to trust him myself.

"Yes, I am. If he comes back, I will let him know that there is a plan for Emma. He could be your way in here."

I hate that he might be right. "How is Sophia doing?"

"She's staying strong but would very much like to get out of here." Michael rubs at the scruff of his beard.

"I can imagine. I'll try to contact you again tomorrow night with more details. Stay safe," I say to him.

"You as well, and take care of my little girl."

"I will," I reply as I exit the dream realm.

I immediately send a group text asking the team to meet me in the dining room. I'm beginning to think our crazy plan of going rogue might just work. Once everybody's seated at the large rectangular table, I tell them all about my visit with Michael, and Maverick writes down all the facts Michael gave me and adds them to the peg board on the wall we're using. There are quite a few shocked faces, but the one that stands out is Sierra's. She's pale and looks like she may pass out.

"Are you okay?" I ask her quietly while the others were talking amongst themselves.

"I'm fine. I want to go with you when we get Emma," she demands.

"I already plan on it. You don't think she would just go with a random stranger, do you?" I ask the obvious question hoping to bring her out of whatever she's thinking.

"They said they were okay, though?" Her hands are fisted together against her stomach.

"Yes, they're fine for now, but we need to get them out of there soon. There's no telling what Excalibur is planning to do."

SIERRA

Later on that evening we finalize our plan for getting Emma to safety. Even though it will break the law, our best path would be to reveal the truth about what we are to Emma. On the one hand, we tell her and break the law, but on the other hand, we save her from being Excalibur's pawn. The High Council can't exactly fault us for that. I can't believe Eric has known. I feel humiliated. He doesn't have the mark of an immortal, so I am guessing Eric's transition wasn't in Graystone.

Well, that will be awkward as hell, trying to work with Eric and Dante together. I still have feelings for Eric, but I would never act on them. Dante is my anima gemella, and I'm in love with him. I feel complete when I'm with Dante, even if he did erase my memories. I know he did what he needed to do, as much as it still stings to think about. When I look into Dante's eyes, I feel a deeper connection than I've ever felt with anybody else.

Does that mean Eric knew about Dante? At least Emma hasn't gone away to college yet, so it shouldn't be too hard to find her. We have to be careful because we don't know if Excalibur has anybody keeping an eye on Emma. Dante and the others decide I should send her a coded text to meet up that only she would know if her phone is being monitored.

I take out my burner phone and text her. "Hey chicky, it's Destiny. Do you want to watch some bratty kids run around?" She called me Destiny when I told her about my first dream about Dante, and while sitting in the cafeteria at the mall, we used to make it a pastime by watching all the crazy antics the kids would do. We would have plenty of visibility in the restaurant and be able to spread out and blend in better. I haven't spoken to Emma since just after the plane crash when I told her I was okay but not to say anything. I knew she had a lot of questions and was worried, but I'm sure Emma will understand why I had to hide the truth. I have really missed her.

Within minutes my phone goes off with a message from Emma. "Hi Destiny, what time are we babysitting tonight?" she replies, clearly getting that it had to be secret.

"We start at seven, and it's an overnight, so I would grab some stuff you may need." I hope she packs like she usually does, a whole suitcase for a sleepover.

"Can't wait!" she replies with a smiley face emoji.

Dante thought it was best to only have himself, Maverick, Roger and me to meet up with Emma. The fewer of us, the more chance of not being visible. Roger is another immortal guardian who has joined us. Roger's brother Arthur is one of the missing immortal guardians that we suspect was also kidnapped by Excalibur many decades ago. Roger seems nice, but he's kind of socially awkward around women. He won't make eye contact with me when we talk. As long as Dante trusts him, I will too. Dante creates a portal to a back parking lot of the mall surrounded by shrubs and trees. Dante and I lead the way, and he instructs the others to wait five minutes before they come around to the front of the mall. Dante and I walk into the mall separately to make it look like we're not together.

Since, we're about twenty minutes early for the meet, I walk into one of the shops close by and pick up a few more clothing items just in case. I have about five minutes to spare, so I head to Joe's Burgers, and I spot Emma at our usual table. I have to remind myself to walk like a normal person and not to run to her. It feels like it's been ages since we've seen each other.

As soon as she spots me, her eyes light up, and she smiles. When I finally get to her table, she stands and wraps me in a hug. We both squeeze hard like we're afraid to let go. I have to wipe the tears from my eyes before anybody sees them.

"Are you okay? I've missed you so much," she asks, looking all over me for signs of injury.

"I'm okay, but there's a lot going on right now. I've missed you so much too. I'm sorry I had to keep you in the dark."

"It's okay. I know you had to have a good reason." We both take our seats.

Within a minute, a waiter comes by to take our order, and we both order a burger and onion rings. As I look around, I'm able to spot Dante at a booth within hearing distance. I also spot Maverick and Roger walking into the cafeteria looking for a place to sit.

"You will not believe everything that I am going to tell you, but I swear it is all true." I look directly into her eyes, hoping she will understand.

"Destiny, whatever you say, I believe you," she says honestly, giggling just a little.

"Okay, well, first of all, don't be obvious but check out the guy in the black shirt and black hat in the booth to your right. That is Dante," I say, watching as realization is setting in that my dreams were actually real.

"Damn girl, he is hot." She smirks.

"I know, right? Listen, I'm going to get right to the point. You have to come with us because it's not safe for you right now."

"Why do you say that?" She cocks her head to the side.

"Well, to be honest, I'm an immortal, and so are my parents and Uncle Joe. There's a really bad immortal out there called Excalibur, and he has my parents as prisoners. He is the one who caused the plane crash." I have to stop talking because the waiter comes back with our food.

When he leaves, I lean over the table. "I hate to be the one to tell you this, but your dad is an immortal as well. He's working with Excalibur, and your mom is human, but she's also helping them. Eric is also an immortal, but he doesn't want to help Excalibur and his growing army. It was forced on him. They've been blackmailing him by saying they'll hurt you if Eric doesn't do what Excalibur wants." I let that sink in for a moment while I took a bite of my cheeseburger.

She stares at me like she's having a hard time processing all of it. Finally, she mumbles, "Shit."

"I'm sorry, I know it's a lot Emma, but I just found out about all of this after the plane crash. It's been quite the emotional rollercoaster for me with my parents being kidnapped and not knowing for a while if they were dead or alive."

"So, my parents are helping the bad guy?" Her hand tightens around her cheeseburger until ketchup leaks out on the sides.

"Yes, unfortunately, they are," I say, feeling bad about it.

"But they became a doctor and a nurse to help people?" she asks, confusion flashing across her face as she shakes her head as if in denial.

"I know, I didn't want to believe it either, but maybe they're being forced to as well. We just don't know yet." I hope that's true. "If we have you someplace safe where any of Excalibur's goons can't find you, we may have a chance to get both our parents back."

"Clearly, I've missed a lot in the few weeks we've been apart." She sinks back against her chair. "If this information was coming from anyone else I wouldn't believe them, but you're my person. I know you wouldn't lie to me." She looks down at her food.

"I will fill you in on everything when we get to a safe place. You'll have to leave your phone behind, though, so they can't track you. Did you pack a bag?"

"I did. But I wasn't sure what to pack, so I may need to grab a few more things. Can I run home first?" she asks me.

I look to Dante, and he shakes his head. "No, we can't but is it something you can get here in the mall? I can buy it for you."

"No, that's okay. I got it. I take it we will be gone for a little while?" she asks.

"Hopefully not too long, but yes it will be a little while," I say as I finish my burger. "You should finish eating so we can get going."

"I'm trying." She glares at me. "But after all your news, my stomach is in knots."

Even with Emma angry, it feels good to be around her again even if our world was falling apart. We both finish our meals and then go to a store to pick up a couple of items Emma still needs. Having Dante close by and keeping an eye on us makes me feel safer. It's strange to be in the normal world now and wondering what or who can be lurking around the next corner.

CHAPTER 19

DANTE

Watching Sierra with Emma reinforces that we made the right call. As I was eating my cheeseburger that Sierra insisted that I must try, I was enjoying her smile and laughter that being around Emma brought.

I watch over the two young women as they shop to make sure nobody is around. Once we have Emma in the safety of our compound I'm going to try to reach out to Eric. I don't particularly like that idea, but he would be a good asset to have strategically speaking. I wonder how deep in the system Excalibur has his people. We will need more immortals to help when we do storm the prison that is holding Michael, Sophia, and who knows how many others.

We go back to our compound, and Sierra goes with Emma to get her settled in a room just down the hall from our own. Emma seems to be taking everything pretty well, which kind of surprises me. Earlier I told Sierra I planned on trying to reach Eric in a dream, and she must have sensed my unease with that.

"As I'm sure your already aware since you know everything about me, I did have a crush on Eric, but I don't want that to come between us." She searched my face to see how I took the news. "I love you with everything I have, and I am not going anywhere. You are my anima gemella. You are the man that I want to be with."

She must have known what I needed to hear. "I love you with every fiber of my being," I said as I kissed her and pressed my body against her.

I can't wait for things to go back to normal again. What would even be normal for us after going rogue? I want to be able to spend time with just Sierra and not have to worry about the world going up in flames. Once I'm ready to reach Eric I grab my stones and settle on the bed. I place my azurite stone in my right hand and my amethyst stone in the left. I can't believe I am trying to channel a guy Sierra once had feelings for. I try to calm my nerves as much as I can in this situation and think about him. Of course, a vision keeps creeping into my mind of him kissing her at Emma's. I actively have to fight to keep that image out.

I figure a safe, neutral spot to create a dream realm would be his parent's front steps. I picture the yellow building with the white trim and the concrete steps leading to the front door. I start constructing the dream. All I have left to do is to focus all of my energy on finding Eric. I finally spot him, and he must have been drinking because his conscious is swaying like Sierra's was when she was drunk. I grab a hold of it and pull him into the dream anyway.

Once he is through, he looks at me and says, "Who the fuck are you?"

"Hello Eric, you don't know me, but my name is Dante. We need to talk."

"You're right. I don't know you, so why would I want to talk to you?"

Wow, this guy really is an ass. It makes me wonder what Sierra could have seen in him in the first place.

"It's about Emma and the predicament you're in. I think we can help each other," I say.

He seems shocked by that little tidbit. "Oh really? And how do I know this isn't some kind of trap?"

"Because I'm Sierra's boyfriend, and you are literally the last person I want to ask for help." The muscle in my jaw twitches as I cross my arms over my chest.

"You're the one that saved her on the plane, aren't you?" he asks, his brow furrowing.

"I am. If not for me, she would've either been taken by Excalibur or died when the plane crashed," I say, trying not to grit my teeth.

"Thank you for saving her. I care about her a lot, and I didn't know they would hurt her." Eric looks down at the sidewalk.

He looks like he's telling the truth, and I want to believe him. I just don't think I can. "It's done now, but we need to get Michael and Sophia back, as well as the other prisoners Excalibur is holding. That's where you come in." I try to smother my anger.

"I can't help, or they'll hurt Emma. She's the only reason I am in this mess in the first place."

"What if I told you, I had Emma? That she's here with Sierra and I. Would you help then?" I raise my eyebrows and cock my head to the side.

He seems to think it over. "Yes, but I would need proof. I'm sorry, but I can't just trust anybody's word on my sister's safety. I need to see her myself to know."

"That's fair enough, and I expected that. I'm going to give you a key that goes to a safety deposit box that is located in the Colorado Federal Credit Union on Main Street. Do you know where that is?"

"Yeah. What will be in the deposit box?"

"There will be a small box wrapped like a present, but do not open it inside the bank. There's a burner phone in there with a pre-programmed phone number. You can face time that phone number and see Emma." I lean against the steel railing.

"Okay, and then?" Eric looks up and makes strong eye contact. For being intoxicated, he is actually level-headed. At least, he's lost much of his anger and cockiness.

"From there, we will discuss how to move forward. I'm counting on your help." I hand him the small key with a small tag that says #45. I'm really hoping he's not completely wasted and he remembers.

"I will go first thing in the morning." Eric flips the key over in his hand.

"We'll talk soon," I say as I pull out of the dream realm.

Back in the real world, I walk down the hall to Emma's room and knock on the door. Sierra is the one that opens it. "Were you able to reach him?" Sierra looks hopeful.

"Yes. He was skeptical and thought it could be a trap which I figured he would think. I gave him the key to the safety deposit box. Hopefully, he'll call first thing in the morning."

Sierra sighs in obvious relief. "That's good news."

We say our goodnights to Emma and return to our room. We will need to get some sleep before he calls tomorrow.

SIERRA

It's nice having Emma here with us. I fill her in on a lot of the things that have happened since we last spoke. I know Dante is uncomfortable with Eric being part of the team, and I don't blame him. I'm not sure how I would handle being around someone he had a crush on. As soon as we wake up, we grab Emma and head downstairs for an early breakfast and sit around the dining room table waiting for Eric to call her.

When he finally does call and finds out Emma is okay, we start swapping information. By this time, Uncle Joe and Maverick have joined us at the table. Maverick is writing down everything as Eric explains how to best get in undetected and the layout of the prison. With Eric's help, we are slowly piecing together a plan to get the prisoners out.

We all agree to contact each other again tomorrow morning. We'll wait for Eric to call us, so we don't blow his cover. I hope that he doesn't get caught trying to help us. I can't stand the thought of anybody getting hurt because of my family's history.

I've been practicing my hydrokinesis gift, and I must say that it's getting easier to control. I owe a good deal of that to Konstantina. She created a beautiful aquamarine ring that I wear on my right ring finger. The stone itself is a translucent pale blue-green like the ocean surrounding us, and the gem is wrapped in a delicate weave of silver wire. She said since my gift is water manipulation, a stone that is tied to the ocean would give me a never-ending supply of energy as well as much-needed help to focus.

I have to really concentrate for my gift to manifest. I've been able to create more water bombs and lift water from the ground. Konstantina said that when she was a child, she was told of folktales of immortals with elemental powers and how closely hydrokinesis can merge into what is called atmokinesis, or manipulation of the weather. She also said there was only one immortal who was ever rumored to have atmokinesis and that was a god.

I'm not really sure how that makes me feel. If she thinks that being able to manipulate the weather will help us against Excalibur, then I'm willing to try. We don't know what we're up against just yet. Eric did shine some light on the number of followers Excalibur has amassed and it is a lot more than we had initially thought. Eric estimated that Excalibur's Revolution involves close to 100 acolytes. We have been able to talk five more into helping us so we are up to a group of sixteen so far not counting humans. That's still a far cry from 100.

With Eric's help we now know where Excalibur's main base is and my dad was right, it is in India. Unfortunately, he has overtaken the Murud Janjira Fort which is completely surrounded by the sea. Eric also informed us that in one week Excalibur is moving to phase three of his master plan, but he doesn't know what that may be. I can't imagine the third step would be good news for the prisoners or us. We plan on infiltrating the compound before phase three begins. That only gives us six full days before we storm the fort.

If we are not enough of a force to eradicate Excalibur and his band of henchmen, I can only hope that we are enough to rescue those that have been captured and held against their will.

The End.

You can find out what happens to Sierra and her friends in the next installment of the Destiny Of Graystone Series, Into The Storm.

About The Author

Katie lives in Vermont with her husband and their children. When she's not working or spending time with her family, she enjoys getting lost in a good book. Her favorite hobby is gardening, whether it's edible or decorative. In her opinion, one can never have too many flowers! She may have a slight addiction to creating things in Canva and Procreate. Visit http://www.katierichard.com for more information and be sure to sign up for her newsletter to stay informed.